Preferential Treatment

Heather Guerre

Preface

Preferential Treatment touches on topics that may be difficult for some readers, including childhood neglect, addiction (side characters), dysfunctional family dynamics, wealth inequality, and poverty. Sexual elements include a D/s femdom relationship.

Chapter One

Kate stared at her computer screen, vaguely aware that an excited murmur had arisen on the far side of the office. She didn't bother standing up to peer over cubicles at the commotion. It was almost certainly because of a food delivery. The only reason anybody ever got excited about anything around here was because there was free food in the break room.

She'd go find out what it was in a second. First, she had a freight issue to deal with. She picked up the phone and punched in the number for her favorite Port Authority contact. He was incredibly susceptible to a bit of flirting, which often allowed Kate to finagle favors that maybe weren't entirely above board, but they made her job a hell of a lot easier.

As she listened to the phone ring, the murmuring commotion drifted closer to her cubicle. She heard the sound of male voices conversing excitedly, their words indistinct. Must be something really good in the break room.

Her regular contact went to voicemail. Uttering a quiet

"shit," she dialed the backup contact—a no-nonsense woman who would inevitably tell Kate to go fuck herself in logistics jargon.

"This is Tammy," she answered abruptly, as she always did.

"Hey Tammy, it's Kate Pasternak with Domovoy Technologies."

"*Kate*, hm? Jeff'll be sorry he missed your call." The snideness was not totally unwarranted. Tammy knew Kate played Jeff like a fiddle, and Kate was evolved enough to recognize that her manipulations probably made Tammy's work more difficult.

It didn't stop her from doing it, though.

"Oh, yeah? Well, tell him hi from me, would you?" Kate replied, ramping up her Wisconsin accent. It had a weird effect on people. The accent itself wasn't particularly attractive, but it led a lot of people to assume she was wholesome and sweet and maybe a little bit dim. It helped smooth the way with more cantankerous types. "Listen, I just got a call from my carrier that you guys are turning freight away? There's got to be something we can do."

"Nope. Try Philly."

Kate looked down at her map. A slight shadow fell across her desk—somebody standing at the opening to her cubicle. She ignored whoever it was. They'd just have to wait. She was busy. "I already contacted Philadelphia and Boston and it's the same story. None of the smaller ports can take a ship this size, and you guys have the most capacity, so if—"

A male hand suddenly appeared in Kate's peripheral vision, reaching for one of the printouts on her desk. Irritated, she caught the intruder by the wrist and flung his hand away.

"Didn't your mother teach you to ask first?" she snapped without looking at the offender.

"*Excuse me?*"

"Sorry, Tammy, not you. I've got somebody grabbing stuff off my desk. Listen, I think if we just..." Kate trailed off as she realized a deathly hush had fallen over the office. Heads popped over cubicle walls like wide-eyed prairie dogs. She swiveled back to look at who she'd just manhandled.

He was unnervingly tall, dressed in an expensive-looking, immaculately-tailored suit. He looked like he was carved from granite—pale skin, tightly cropped dark brown hair, thick black brows over hooded eyes so dark she couldn't tell the iris from the pupil. His features were starkly cast, with a bold, Roman nose, prominent cheekbones, and a sharply carved jawline. He wasn't handsome exactly, but he was definitely striking. That harsh face was set in a cold, unreadable mask as he looked Kate over. One hand gripped his other wrist—the wrist Kate had caught and flung away—rubbing it as if he'd been burned.

Fuck.

It was Mikhail Volkov. The CEO, majority shareholder, and founder of Domovoy Technologies. Kate had never met him before, but she'd seen his picture often enough to recognize him immediately. He was one of the richest, most powerful men in the world. And she'd just grabbed him and scolded him like a bratty child.

Welp. So much for this job.

She closed her eyes briefly as she let out a resigned sigh. When she opened them again, she straightened her spine and lifted her chin. "Tammy? Sorry, I'm going to have to call you back." She hung up and when she stood up to face him, Mikhail Volkov was leaning against her cubical divider, surveying her critically, his wintery Russian unreadability still in full force.

"Kate!" Her ridiculously young department head stood nervously behind the CEO, looking like he wanted to faint dead away. "Have you met Mikhail Volkov? Um, Mikhail—" he said the man's name uncertainly, as if he weren't sure he had the right "—this is Kate Pasternak. She's one of our logistics coordinators for overseas freight."

"Pasternak?" Mikhail echoed, pronouncing it with proper Slavic inflection, rather than the Anglicized way Kate pronounced her own surname. "Russian?"

Kate hesitated for a second, not sure why they were going through the ruse of small-talk when she was obviously about to get reamed out. "Polish," she answered stiffly. "On my dad's side."

Mikhail stared at her for a moment longer, stone-faced, saying nothing.

Kate raised her eyebrows. She hated these stupid intimidation games. "Can I help you with anything else?" She let an edge of impatience bleed into the frosty professionalism of her tone. After manhandling and snapping at the CEO, she was definitely going to be fired. No sense in licking his boots on her way out.

Mikhail pushed away from the divider, straightening to his full height, expression unchanging. "I would like to see you in my office in one hour, Ms. Pasternak." His deep-voiced accent lent an intimidating touch to the softly-spoken words.

The urge to quit on the spot—to refuse to let her fate rest in the hands of some dispassionate, entitled, billionaire asshole—almost won out. But common sense managed to take over, and she remained just as stone-faced as the man staring back at her.

"Alright," she answered coolly. "I'll see you in an hour."

Without another word, Mikhail Volkov turned and left. The department head cast a crazed look over his shoulder at Kate before hurrying to catch up to the CEO.

When they were out of sight, she sank back down into her chair, staring blankly at her computer screens. She was fucked. Completely and totally. She was already struggling to make rent after her roommate up and ditched her two months ago. Now she was going to be out of work, forced to get by on whatever measly sum unemployment insurance amounted to, applying for new jobs without being able to provide a good reference from her previous workplace.

In the hour she spent waiting to go up to the CEO's office, she got absolutely zero work done. What was the point? Her thoughts circled frantically as she tried to put together a contingency plan for being fired. She'd have to file for unemployment right away—if she even qualified for it. And if she did, would it be enough to keep her from getting evicted? She was already living paycheck-to-paycheck, paying for groceries and smaller necessities with a credit card so that she'd have enough left in checking to pay rent and utilities at the end of the month.

By the time she got up from her desk, her hands were sweaty and her heart was pounding. She gathered her things so that she wouldn't have to do the walk of shame back to her cubicle afterward. Her purse was lumpy and heavy on her shoulder, stuffed near to bursting with her favorite mug, a framed photo of her and her best friend Anna on a girls trip in Door County, the pretty glazed cup she used as a pen holder, and all of the snacks she kept in her bottom desk drawer. She had to drape the multitude of vines from her pothos over her shoulders so they wouldn't drag on the floor while she carried the pot.

A few people cast wary glances at her as she passed their cubicles, quickly looking away as soon as she made eye contact with them. *Cowards*, she sneered inwardly, even as her own knees trembled with each step. She went to the elevator and pressed the button for the top floor.

At the top, the elevator opened into a space that made the rest of the building look like a prison. No low-pile gray carpeting here. No sterile white walls, or speckled drop-panel ceilings, or fluorescent tube lighting. It was all glossy wood floors and textured wallpaper and elegant brass light sconces and big, bright windows overlooking the downtown.

A receptionist's desk dominated the space, backed by a long wall of floor-to-ceiling windows. The receptionist was a middle-aged woman with a sleek Domovoy earpiece in one ear, her attention focused on a Domovoy ultra-slim monitor. She looked up as Kate stepped out of the elevator, her gaze dropping to the potted plant in Kate's hands. A brief flash of confusion crossed her face, but she quickly smoothed it away with a professional, unassuming smile.

"Can I help you?" she asked.

"I'm here to see Mr. Volkov. He's expecting me." Kate's voice came out impressively steady.

The receptionist looked at her monitor, clicking a couple of times. "Kate Pasternak?"

"Yes."

"He's ready for you. Right this way."

The receptionist led her down a hall past a glass-enclosed conference room and several offices with brass placards and frosted-glass doors. The door at the very end was ajar. The receptionist knocked lightly on it, peeking her head into the office.

"Mr. Volkov? Ms. Pasternak is here to see you."

"Thank you. Send her in," that deep, Russian-accented voice drifted from the office, ominously soft.

Tightening her sweaty grip on her potted plant, Kate nodded her thanks to the receptionist and stepped inside. The door shut crisply behind her—the seal on her demise.

Mikhail Volkov's office was just as elegant as the rest of the top floor. A broad wooden desk sat in front of an entire wall of floor-to-ceiling windows, out of which the CEO could look across the rooftops of neighboring downtown buildings to a gorgeous view of the lake.

To the right of the desk, highly polished burled wood cabinets and shelves lined one wall, filled with books and random decor. To the left of the desk, there was a sitting area with a leather chesterfield sofa and two green velvet club chairs arranged around a transparent pedestal coffee table with swirls of golden mica suspended in its surface. The eclecticism could've looked like a cheap attempt to cobble together thrift store furniture, but even to Kate's broke ass, it looked outrageously expensive. Not only the price of the furniture, but also the undoubtedly exorbitant fee charged by the interior designer who'd put it all together.

Standing amidst all this wealth in a thrifted DKNY dress that she'd had to dye black to hide the stain that had come with it, and Target-brand black pumps with a wobbly left heel, Kate felt every dollar of her inferiority piling on top of her. Millions and millions of dollars—*billions*—crushing down on her until she could barely breathe.

"Ms. Pasternak," Mikhail Volkov greeted her in that deep, soft, Russian-inflected voice. His gaze landed on the potted plant in her hands and the vines wrapped around her neck like some bizarre kind of scarf. His thick, dark brows drew together. "Er... please make yourself comfortable." He gestured at the chairs in front of his desk.

"No, I don't think I will," Kate said coldly. She couldn't help herself. She was choking on the unfairness of it all, and she couldn't find it in herself to be sensible and tactful. Her pride wouldn't allow it. "I know why I'm here. Why don't we just get it over with?"

Volkov's brows rose. "Get what over with?"

It was then that Kate realized it was only the two of them in the room. Her direct supervisor wasn't there. Nor was there a human resources representative. She'd have expected both those people present while she was being personally fired by the CEO.

So... maybe she *wasn't* being fired?

"I suppose you want an apology from me," she said, wincing internally at the venom in her tone. Jesus Christ, who needed enemies when she was this good at self-sabotage?

A small, private smile quirked the firm line of his mouth. "On the contrary, I never want to hear an apology from you."

"You... what?" Kate frowned. "Then why am I here?"

He leaned forward, elbows on his desk, fingers steepled together. He was a big man, and the way his suit stretched across his broad shoulders felt like a threat. Through the windows behind him, the rising sun backlit him like an operatic villain. He exuded the cold charisma that came with absurd wealth and unchecked power.

Kate couldn't help but curl her lip at the sight.

His cold, dark eyes gleamed, for the first time, with a hint of interest. "I have a proposition for you."

Chapter Two

Pride and indomitability radiated off of her like an ancient Slavic goddess. It didn't help that the sun coming through the windows had cast her in a pool of morning light, turning her hair the color of old gold, making her eyes snap like blue flames, while she was wrapped in twisting vines and glaring at him like she'd smite him off the face of the earth, given the slightest provocation. Wary and brittle, she might have been a defeated goddess, but she was all the more dangerous for it.

Mikhail shifted slightly in his seat, resisting the need to reach down and readjust himself. He didn't normally respond to a woman so viscerally—at least, not without more pointed inducement. But this woman, just by instinct, had set him on fire in a way that he hadn't felt in a very long time. The pressure of her hand around his wrist was a lingering ghost that he could still feel. Her undiluted scorn when he'd overstepped her bounds was still a hot simmer beneath his skin. Calling her here had been an erratic impulse. Mikhail did not generally surrender to impulse.

His needs, such as they were, went through long dormancies. He could go months, even years, without wanting a woman. But eventually, that need would reawaken, and the urge to satisfy it was all-consuming. With most women, he could burn through the desire in a matter of days, content to be over with it and alone again for a long time. Some women lasted longer, teasing out his needs with practiced skill, keeping his fire stoked for months at a time. But in every case, the arousal preceded the woman. He felt the urge, and then he sought a suitable companion to satisfy it.

With this woman, it had been entirely backwards. It'd been more than a year since he'd last succumbed to his libido, and there'd been no signs that his comfortable celibacy was going to be disrupted any time soon. But then her hand, finely wrought and unexpectedly strong, had closed around his wrist, and lightning had shot straight to his cock, reawakening him with a brutal vengeance. He'd never wanted any particular woman. He'd only ever needed the services they provided. But in the hour since she'd grabbed him, Kate Pasternak had consumed Mikhail's mind to a maddening, inescapable degree.

"A proposition?" Her frown deepened. She didn't fidget or flush or fill the silence with uncomfortable chatter. She simply stared him down, cool and regal, demanding an answer with the cut of her gaze.

"Yes." He didn't elaborate further, curious to see how she would react.

A flash of annoyance crossed her face, but she quickly dampened it. "I'm not being fired?" she demanded, with none of the humility he might reasonably expect to hear in such a question.

"Why would you be fired?"

A humorless smile pulled at one corner of her red-painted mouth. "Are you enjoying this game?"

God, she was perfect.

"Forgive me," he said, indulging himself just a little by imagining himself as a supplicant to her vengeful goddess. "You're right. Let me be straightforward. I have a proposition for you. It is a sensitive topic, and for that reason, I am offering payment in exchange for your discretion in the matter."

Some of the scornful pride faded from her eyes, replaced by confusion. "What?"

"Regardless of your answer to my proposition, I will pay you to keep this conversation between the two of us. Name your price."

The scorn returned. "You're fucking with me."

"I assure you that I am not. Name your price."

She stared at him for a long moment, skeptical and distrustful. "Five thousand dollars," she said, clearly throwing out what she thought was an unreasonable sum.

"That's selling yourself short," he replied. "Let's make it ten thousand."

The skepticism in her eyes deepened. Sunlight glided over her features as she strode towards him, gaze locked with his, searching for a lie. She stopped just in front of the desk, disbelief and distrust written in her expression. Mikhail leaned back, straightening his spine under her perusal. He picked up his phone and called his personal assistant, putting the call on speaker.

"Yes, Mr. Volkov?" she answered in her usual brisk, professional tone.

"Sarah, arrange for ten thousand dollars to be transferred

from my personal discretionary account to whichever account Kate Pasternak deposits her paychecks."

"It will take me a minute. Would you like me to call back when it's done?"

"Just a confirmation text will be fine. Send one to the number we have on file for Ms. Pasternak as well."

"Will do. Anything else, Mr. Volkov?"

"No. That will be all, thank you." He closed the call, raising his eyebrows at the woman standing before him.

In the hour since he'd seen her, he'd done his research. Katrina Rose Pasternak—thirty years old, never married, no children. Born in Antigo, Wisconsin. Associate's degree in logistics, with a technical certificate in supply chain management. Thirty-four grand in credit card debt, a little over eleven grand tied up in a personal loan, and nearly twelve grand in medical debt. An apartment, where she lived alone, whose rent outstripped her means.

She was a woman who suited his needs perfectly. And he was a man who could meet hers—at least where money was concerned.

She narrowed her eyes as she considered him. "Ten thousand dollars for a yes or no question?"

He nodded.

She was quiet, thinking. He waited, tense with anticipation.

Finally, she laughed, half-skeptical, half-amused. "Sure. Ask away."

He gestured at the chairs again. "Won't you sit? Please?"

She considered it, then shrugged. Setting the plant down on his desk, she carefully unwound the vines from her neck and shoulders, and then settled into the nearest chair, back straight, gaze level.

A soft buzz came from the bag she'd set on the floor. Mikhail smiled. "Check your messages."

Giving him a dubious look, she reached into her bag and pulled out her phone. She stared at the screen for a long moment. When she finally looked up, her expression had shifted from skeptical to contemplative.

"The funds have been transferred?" Mikhail asked.

"All ten thousand," she answered, faintly wary.

"Then we are in agreement? The details of this conversation will not leave this office?"

"Alright." She shifted, crossing her legs, leaning forward, and meeting his gaze. "Ask your ten-thousand-dollar question."

Her command crept over his skin like trailing fingers. "Yes. Well. To be blunt, I would like to offer you financial compensation in exchange for your physical companionship."

She blinked, going still as a statue. But she didn't recoil. Didn't gasp in outrage or shock. Didn't leap up and run for the door. A heavy silence descended, seemingly endless. But Mikhail didn't break it. It was one of the oldest rules of negotiations—whoever spoke first lost. And he never lost.

Finally, Kate yielded. "How much?"

Got her. Mikhail kept his expression remote. "In the past, I have—"

She snorted, her gaze flattening with distaste. "Done this a lot, have you?"

"I'm a busy man. I don't have time for relationships. This is a simple arrangement, no gray areas, no hurt feelings, where we both get our needs met." He shrugged.

"Hmm."

Her skepticism wasn't promising, but he wasn't worried.

He continued on. "I have found it simplest to 'gift' my companion on a weekly basis. How do you feel about twenty-five hundred?"

Kate looked at him like he was insane. Maybe he was. "Twenty-five hundred dollars a *week?*" she repeated incredulously. "Just to... what? Fuck you?"

"Not enough?" He tilted his head, considering. He could afford to pay more—far more. But he had to take longevity into account—the more he paid her, the sooner she would no longer need the funds, and the more likely she was to end the arrangement before he was ready for it to be over. It was a careful balancing act between offering enough to be lucrative, but not so much that he shot himself in the foot. The severance pay when he was done with her would more than make up for it. "Five thousand, then?"

Unexpectedly, her skepticism only deepened. It was unusual for anyone to doubt him where money was concerned.

"Five thousand. For *sex*. With *me*."

"Yes."

She sighed. "You're into really weird stuff, aren't you?"

Mikhail shrugged. "Some people would consider it strange." Especially for a man of his position.

She rubbed at her forehead, agitated. "I can't believe I'm entertaining this idea."

Mikhail could believe it. She needed money. He had more money than anyone could ever need. It was a win-win situation. She would say yes. He knew she would.

"What happens to me if I say no?"

"Nothing. If you say no, then the ten thousand dollars is still yours, this conversation never happened, and we continue with our lives as if we'd never met."

She was quiet, looking past him as she contemplated. After a tense silence, she straightened, meeting his gaze again. Hers was unnervingly direct. "Alright, let's rip the bandaid off. Tell me what you're into. Hurting me?"

"No. Not hurting *you*."

The meaningful emphasis gave her pause. After a second, her eyes widened. "*Ah*. That's... not what I expected." She settled into the chair more comfortably. Her sudden ease filled him with victorious elation. "So, you're a masochist?" she asked.

He shook his head. "Not precisely. Pain for pain's sake is not my pleasure."

"Then what *is* your pleasure?"

He had to fight a grin. He must've looked feral, but the wild risk of propositioning her this way—when Mikhail *never* took wild risks—had his adrenaline up. "That is a more detailed conversation that I would prefer not to have in my office. But speaking broadly, when I have the free time to indulge, I would like your company."

Kate said nothing and her face revealed none of her thoughts.

"Within reason, of course. I have obligations and responsibilities that can't be interfered with, and I'm sure you do as well. But aside from that..."

"How often?"

Mikhail shrugged. "My schedule is erratic, depending on the needs of the company. I might spend weeks out of the country, and then have ten days straight of availability. I know your work schedule, and I'm sure you've got obligations outside of work, but if you're willing to be generous with your time for me, I will be generous with my wealth."

He might have misstepped with that one. Kate's eyes

flashed ice cold. She wasn't his usual sort of companion, he had to remind himself. She hadn't come to him intending to make an arrangement. Her dominance wasn't a performance, it was innate. If he insulted her, she'd walk.

He couldn't let her go.

"Please," he said gently, beseechingly. "Let me be generous to you."

She regarded him stonily. Silence stretched between them again, heavy and tense. He heard the ticking of the antique clock on his bookshelf, the rush of wind around the building, the distant sounds of traffic, the rasp of his own breath...

Finally, Kate spoke. "Let's assume I said yes. What happens next?"

"Before either of us commit to anything, it would be best to get safety precautions out of the way."

Her brow furrowed. "What precautions?"

"Just a simple NDA and very routine STI testing. This afternoon, I'm flying out to Seoul. I will be out of the country for two weeks. In that time, I would appreciate it if you had an STI test done. I have not had a partner since my most recent test, but I will get another one done and I will have those results sent to you. I will also have the NDA sent to you. You'll have the two weeks to consider it before signing."

"You're very pragmatic." It did not sound like a compliment. It sounded a bit like she was mocking him.

He shrugged. "I try to be. Is any of that objectionable to you?"

She was slow to answer, searching his face. He knew she would find nothing to read in his expression. "I guess not," she finally said.

"Use these two weeks to think about it. When I return to

Chicago, you can meet me at my house where we will discuss the particulars."

"Your house?" She seemed surprised.

"It's private, accessible, and I know the staff are trustworthy."

She had her elbow propped on her crossed knee, chin resting in her hand. She tapped contemplatively at her upper lip as she searched his face. "I really want to believe you're not going to skin me and turn me into a lampshade."

"If I wanted to turn women into furniture, I can assure you that I would be far more discreet than this."

Kate actually smiled at him. "That was incredibly fucking creepy. Especially with the stoic Russian thing you've got going on." She shook her head. "But, also… weirdly convincing. Alright. I'll come to your house."

Mikhail leaned back in his chair, smiling openly now. Every day he was more convinced—money *could* buy happiness.

Chapter Three

"Alright, this one's a cooperative game, so we'll be playing *together* instead of against each other." Kate's best friend, Anna Teague, shot Kate and Theo—Anna's brother—incriminating looks.

Lost in thought, Kate didn't immediately react. It had been a week since Mikhail Volkov's proposition. The NDA was still sitting on her coffee table, rumpled from multiple readings, but unsigned. In one more week, she would have to make her decision. Every moment that she wasn't actively concentrating on something else, her mind was on *him*.

Since his proposition, she'd been obsessively searching his name. While there were a few inconsequential tabloid items, most of his coverage was about the groundbreaking innovations he'd made in computer hardware, the growth of his company, his elevation from behind-the-scenes computer engineer to billionaire tech magnate in the space of a decade, and a million iterations of the capitalist fairytale of how he, an impoverished and unconnected immigrant, made good on the "American dream." There was nothing about scorned lovers, restraining orders, domestic assault allegations, or mysteriously vanished exes. In fact, there was nothing about any women at all.

When Kate realized Anna was looking at her, and that she had just been sitting there, blank-faced, she rewound the words that had just been spoken. Their meaning clicked, and Kate arrowed a wounded look back at her friend while Theo smirked shamelessly. Quite a few games had been stricken from their "friendly" game nights either because Kate ran the board through superior strategy, or Theo did through underhanded trickery.

Settlers of Catan had been banned because Theo had decided to hoard all the wheat and create a captive market wherein everybody else had to barter at Theo's absurd prices in order to make any progress on their own roads and settlements. Anna had tried to implement rules that prevented resource hoarding, but Kate had immediately recognized the pattern of returns Anna's rules created and adjusted her gameplay in anticipation, winning game after game until Theo had finally caught onto her strategy and disrupted it by focusing all his efforts into building roads that hemmed Kate's settlements in.

According to Anna, Theo and Kate were the only ones having any fun. So, *Settlers of Catan* was out. As were *Agricola, Rising Sun, Small World,* and *Gaia Project,* for similar reasons. Last week, they'd tried *Taboo,* but Anna's fiancé, Jason—the size of a mountain and about as talkative as one—had looked like he was being waterboarded every time it was his turn to give clues. Meanwhile, Theo and Kate had banded together, absolutely destroying everybody else.

The new game went well enough. The nature of the play prevented Theo and Kate from railroading everyone else.

Theo was obviously bored by it. Kate didn't necessarily mind the idea of collaborative play, but it did remind her a little bit of being forced to do group work in school. Waiting for the others to take their turns bordered on excruciating. Jason's cousin Zach was a nice enough guy, but he kept getting derailed by pointless details that made Kate want to snatch the dice out of his hands. And his wife, Mel, kept forgetting key details that had already been established, making moves that got them nowhere. At several points, Kate had to stop herself from barking out "NO!" to Mel's moves.

On the bright side, it took her focus off of Mikhail Volkov. At least for a little while.

Later, when the game was done and everyone was just chatting, Kate went into the kitchen for another drink. Anna and Theo were in there, bickering. The two siblings somehow looked exactly like each other, and yet totally different. Both had fawn-colored hair and hazel-brown eyes. Both had the same slightly aquiline nose. They even had the same crooked smile that pulled one corner of their mouth higher than the other. But Anna's features were softer, more doe-eyed, and she looked like doves might land on her shoulders if she started singing. Meanwhile, Theo was a sharp-edged, nearly gaunt, recovering addict, and he exuded the sort of feral energy that made strangers instinctively avoid eye contact with him.

"—good at what she does," Anna was saying earnestly. "Just give it a shot. You're getting everything together and this could really—

"I'm not your charity project, Annie," Theo said tiredly. "Let me handle—" He cut himself off when he noticed Kate. He shot a quelling look at his sister and left the kitchen. Anna watched him go with a resigned sigh.

Kate chose not to comment. She opened the fridge and pulled out a can of soda, wiggling it in Anna's direction. "You want anything?"

"No, I'm good. Oh—hey! I have a question for you."

Kate straightened abruptly. Irrationally, she halfway believed that Anna knew about the offer from Mikhail Volkov. But how could she? It was impossible. And yet, Anna always seemed to know these things. It was like she had some sort of prophetic sense for other people's troubles.

"Uh... what?" Kate asked hesitantly.

"Are you still looking for a roommate?"

Kate relaxed. "Oh, that."

Anna's brows rose. "*That?* What else would it be? Got something on your mind?"

"No."

Anna narrowed her eyes. Kate imagined a psychic shield around her brain, blocking Anna's unnatural perceptiveness. Of course mind-reading wasn't real. But it didn't hurt to take precautions.

"Hm." Anna's suspicion faded with a shrug. "Well, anyway, a friend of mine is moving to Chicago, and she's looking for a roommate."

Kate leaned against the fridge, thinking. *Did* she need a roommate? The ten-thousand dollars from Mikhail would cover a hypothetical roommate's half of the rent for nearly a year. But if Kate got a roommate *now*, she could use that money to pay down her credit-card debt instead.

But, if she took Mikhail up on his offer, she'd have more money coming in every week, and wouldn't necessarily need a roommate. She had to consider, though, how long the arrangement would even last. He wasn't exactly proposing marriage, here. And what if she didn't take the offer at all?

She needed the money, but her pride had some value too, and being a billionaire's on-call sugar baby rankled a little bit. She'd always imagined herself manning the guillotine during the revolution, not jerking off the ruling the class.

"Yeah, actually, I am. Who's this friend?"

"She was my best friend growing up," Anna said.

Kate instinctively bristled with jealousy, but she kept her expression mild.

"She's been sober for almost a year—" Anna continued.

"*Anna*," Kate sighed, exasperated. "What is it with you and addicts?"

"Hey," Anna chided softly. "If you don't want her as a roommate, you can say so. But people struggle sometimes, and they deserve help when they're trying to get better."

Unmoved by Anna's saintliness, Kate crossed her arms. "Am I going to have to worry that this friend of yours is going to steal all my shit so she can sell it for a fix when she relapses?"

"No. If she relapsed, most likely she'd just disappear on you."

Kate started to reply, but Anna cut her off.

"*But*, I don't think she's going to relapse. Her problem's with alcohol, not drugs. And her drinking was a coping mechanism. Moving here is the next step in escaping the environment that she had to cope with."

Kate considered that. Anna was a bleeding heart, but she had an unnervingly good sense of people. "Alright," she finally said. "Give your friend my number. We'll talk and see if we fit."

Anna smiled brightly, coming over to wrap Kate in a tight hug. "You act tough, but you're a big softie," she said.

Kate squeezed Anna back in an aggressive bear hug, crushing the air out of her lungs. "No I'm not. Take it back."

Anna jabbed Kate in the ribs—right in her most ticklish spot. With a shriek, Kate released her.

"Illegal move!" she gasped, clapping a protective hand over the tender spot.

"Softie." Anna smirked and then dashed back into the dining room where she could use her mountainous fiancé as a shield.

"Chicken!" Kate called after her, grinning.

But then she was alone in the kitchen, just her and her thoughts, and the smile faded. She picked at the tab on the soda can as her mind returned immediately to Mikhail. She still didn't know what she was going to do.

She was a little afraid to find out.

Chapter Four

Mikhail Volkov's Chicago home was a beautiful old Romanesque-style mansion in Lincoln Park, with a facade of gray limestone accented with red brick. A curving stone portico framed the double front doors. A rounded turret clung to the opposite corner of the house. A high stone wall surrounded the property, enclosing a yard shaded with graceful old oaks, gray and leafless in late winter.

Kate sat in silence in the back of a sleek black Bentley, trying not to let her nerves show. The driver pulled onto the cobbled driveway, stopping in front of a wrought iron gate to wave an ID card over the security scanner. The gates slid open and the car rolled smoothly onto the property, passing beneath the elegant portico before circling around to the back of the house. Everything about the house proclaimed the resident's wealth—from the architecture, to the age, to the size. The magnificent house seemed to loom over Kate, the windows like too many blank eyes, staring down at her, unimpressed.

Trying to project the illusion that she wasn't totally out of her depth, she sat with patient dignity while the driver came around to open her door. When she stepped out onto the cobbles, a thin, gray-haired man in a crisp white button-down shirt and pleated navy slacks emerged from a side door. He stood beneath a copper-domed overhang, awaiting her. Was she being shown in through the servants' entrance? What was this, Downton Abbey?

"Hello, Ms. Pasternak. I'm David Marx. I'm Mr. Volkov's household manager."

Oh, Jesus Christ. The man had a butler. This *was* Downton Abbey. "Nice to meet you, Mr. Marx," Kate said, trying to sound unfazed.

"Call me David. Mr. Volkov is in a conference call right now, but if you'll follow me this way?"

He led Kate inside, stepping into a small marble-floored entryway with dark mahogany wainscoting and an art nouveau chandelier overhead with sculpted brass arms that looked like leaves and vines, and frosted glass flowers as shades around the bulbs.

God, if this was the humble side-entry, what the hell did the main entryway look like?

David took Kate's coat and scarf, hanging them up just around the corner before leading her in the opposite direction. She followed him down a long hallway lined with leaded-glass windows that overlooked the side yard. Now, the yard was covered in snow, but an arching trellis indicated that it was probably a beautiful garden in the warmer seasons. Beneath Kate's clicking steps, the wooden floor gleamed like polished glass, with multiple tones of wood inlaid in an elaborate parquet that rivaled a Turkish rug for complexity.

They rounded the corner at the end of the hall, and at a pair of glass-paned french doors, David showed her into a plush sitting room. In a house like this, Kate supposed it would be called a "parlor" or "receiving room" or something like that. The far wall was all floor-to-ceiling windows that overlooked the backyard. Despite being covered in snow, the signs of a beautiful garden were strongly evident, with arbors and hedges and a multi-tiered stone fountain.

The room itself was comfortably—but expensively—furnished with plushly upholstered chairs and a tufted loveseat. The side tables and coffee table were all antiques of different eras, and were obviously valuable pieces. One wall was dominated by a large Victorian-era fireplace with a decorative tile surround and a large wooden mantle. Elegant, peaceful art hung on the walls—an oil painting of a forested landscape, a watercolor study of a vividly-colored bird's wing, a huge wooden clock with hanging chains and a big brass pendulum, a circular brass-framed mirror with a floral border etched around the edges of the glass.

In anticipation of having to stand amidst Mikhail's obvious wealth, Kate had worn her favorite dress—a vintage black sheath dress that fit like a glove. It was a seventies-era dress that she'd found in a heap of clothes at an estate sale. She'd snagged it for fifty dollars, which felt almost unethical after she'd looked the couturier up online and found other dresses selling on second-hand sites for hundreds of dollars.

But even dressed to kill, Kate felt like a grubby peasant standing in the King's court. She took in all the details of the house—the furnishings, the surrounding neighborhood—and knew without a doubt that she did not belong here, and everyone who saw her would know it.

Compared to the trailers she grew up in, her current

apartment would be considered obscenely lavish, with its high ceilings and crown molding and vintage maple floors. But *this* house? It was as inconceivable as a fairytale castle. She tried to picture her family standing in it and immediately cringed with embarrassment. Luckily, David didn't see.

"Can I get you any refreshment?" he offered as he stepped to the side of the doorway, subtly gesturing for Kate to enter the room.

"No," she said faintly. "Thank you."

David nodded an acknowledgment. "Then, if you'll make yourself comfortable, Mr. Volkov should be ready for you in a moment."

"Thank you."

Kate sank into the nearest chair, giving her a view out the window, while the doorway remained in her peripheral vision. The house was so big, so still. Despite being alone, she felt like there was a spotlight on her. She resisted the urge to reach for her phone. Instead, she kept her hands folded over her crossed legs and stared out the window. Little birds fluttered and hopped around the nicest bird feeders Kate had ever seen, leaving seed hulls and tiny little birdie footprints in the snow. Squirrels chased each other along the top of the stone perimeter wall. More birds mingled in the branches of the dormant trees, fluffed up against the cold.

A few minutes passed in that wary stillness, but she kept her thoughts off of what she was actually doing here, and just focused on the birds. Motion in the corner of her eye pulled her attention to the doorway. She expected to see David, coming to escort her to Mikhail perhaps, but the man in the doorway was too tall, too broad, too intimidating to be the circumspect, elder "household manager."

It was Mikhail. He looked just as coldly indifferent as he

had two weeks ago. His black gaze swept over her, betraying nothing of his thoughts.

"Ms. Pasternak," he greeted her, pronouncing her name with that Russian inflection. His voice was deep, a little gravelly, but totally professional. An outside viewer could easily mistake this for a business meeting of some sort.

Well. That's what it was, at its core, wasn't it? He wanted to pay her for services rendered.

Kate rose from her seat to face him, keeping her expression just as unreadable as his. "Mr. Volkov," she returned, just as politely. "How was Seoul?"

He tilted his head from side to side, an indecisive gesture. "Busy," he finally said. "Would you come to my office? We can speak privately there."

"Lead the way."

His office was upstairs, on the second story. The wooden floor was less elaborately parqueted than the downstairs hallways, but a gorgeous, jewel-toned oriental rug covered most of it. The far wall was filled with wooden shelves, stuffed with books. Two button-tufted leather chairs sat before a wide, polished, mahogany desk, behind which, a sleek leather desk chair sat. Another colorful rug covered the wall behind the desk, a design choice that struck Kate as very Russian. To the left of the desk, a row of tall, narrow, leaded-glass windows overlooked the backyard. Kate's glance was drawn there for just a moment, landing on the birds. Their simple presence steadied her.

"Please, take a seat," Mikhail gestured to the chairs.

Kate didn't want to sit. Even when they were both standing, he towered over her. Despite the fact that she was a relatively tall woman, and she was wearing heels, she still had to tilt her head a bit to meet his gaze. If she sat, he'd seem like a giant. Instead, she propped her hip against the desk, placing her purse on it, and crossed her arms, giving him a bold once-over.

He was dressed more casually than he'd been at the office two weeks ago, wearing charcoal gray dress pants and a pale blue oxford shirt with the sleeves rolled up to his elbows. He stood still under her blatant perusal, hands in his pockets, gaze locked on her face.

"*You* sit," she said, using her foot to push out the chair in front of her.

To her surprise, he acquiesced. When he sank down, stoic face tilted up to her, that looming feeling faded, and suddenly Kate could relax.

"Alright. We're speaking privately now. You made it clear this is a sexual arrangement. What exactly do you want from me?"

A flicker of some emotion passed over his face, too quickly for her to read. "It's not what *I* want from *you*. It's what you want from me."

Kate frowned. "That would be...?"

"Anything," he said flatly. "Anything you want. I would be yours to command and control. To reward when I please you and to punish when I do not."

Kate found that hard to believe. He radiated dominance and power. It was evident in the flintiness of his gaze, the confidence in his posture, the comfort with which he occupied the world. There was nothing deferential, nothing servile, in the way he looked at her now. She could believe that he enjoyed a woman taking sexual initiative, but she doubted very much that he liked being told what to do otherwise.

Testing her theory, she said softly, "Get on your knees."

Without hesitation, he eased his big body from the chair to kneel at Kate's feet. He looked up at her, hands resting on his thick thighs, just the faintest hint of something dangerous glimmering in those cold, remote eyes.

"Hands behind your back," she said.

He obeyed, clasping them together behind him. There was no resentment in his gaze, no stubborn pride, no rebellion. Just quiet interest. He was simply waiting for whatever came next.

"What if I told you to stay like this for an hour?"

"Then I would obey you," he answered readily.

"What if I told you to stay like this for an hour, then I went home, and that was the end of it? No sex. No gratification."

He licked his lips. His gaze darkened. "Then I would obey you."

She raised her brows, skeptical, and let the silence speak for her.

"*Although*," he relented, "I would prefer to serve you more actively. To make you come."

Her brows rose higher.

"As often as you wanted. Whenever you wanted."

Kate sank back against the desk, taking that in. Her gaze traveled over him—Mikhail Volkov, the powerful tech billionaire, kneeling at the feet of some Midwestern trailer-trash nobody, asking to make her come—wanting to *pay* for the privilege to do so.

This couldn't be real. And yet, she had ten grand sitting in her checking account that said otherwise.

"Why me?" she asked. The question came out too raw, unguarded. She quickly schooled her expression back into dispassionate calm. "Why not hire a professional? A man of your means could have anybody in the world."

"Yes, I could," he agreed, a touch of arrogance hardening that cool mask. "But there are women to whom this comes naturally, and that's what I want."

"You think this comes naturally to me?" She wasn't sure if she was offended or not.

"Command? Self-possession? A complete disregard for my authority?" A faint smile tilted the corner of his mouth. "Yes. I think those things come naturally to you. There are plenty of women who'd be happy to play the part, but that's all it would be—a performance. Not *real* dominance." The last few words slipped out with more emotion than she'd yet heard from him. Hunger and need. The heat of them washed over Kate, warming her deep inside.

She took a second to steady herself, licking her lips. Mikhail's dark eyes tracked the movement. The cold mask fell away entirely, revealing a raw combination of hunger, pleasure, wistfulness.

"Please," he said softly. That deep, graveled, Russian accent coasted over her senses like the rasp of calloused hands. Mikhail's eyes searched her face, growing heated as he observed her response. "Please, knyazhna. Own me."

He gazed up at her, still on his knees, hands still clasped behind his back. His shirt strained across his broad shoulders and chest, while his thighs tested the confines of his trousers. He was big and strong and so harshly masculine—and he was kneeling at Kate's feet, relinquishing all that power to her.

It was difficult to focus with that appealing offer laid before her, but she needed to think. She was tempted to accept the offer, regardless of the money, simply on the grounds that she *wanted* this.

But he was her boss. And not just her boss, but the founder and CEO of the entire company. And he wasn't just some plebeian *millionaire* CEO. He was one of the richest men in the world, his net worth over fifty billion. No matter how much power he handed over to Kate, she was still the one with everything to lose.

Even so, the money was an unholy temptation. She didn't technically *need* it anymore. He wasn't firing her from her job, so she'd still have her regular income. And after talking to Anna's friend Naomi on the phone, she'd agreed to a roommate arrangement, starting next week, so she no longer had to worry about covering all of the rent on her own. But she was still living with a mountain of debt, and the amount of money Mikhail was offering—five grand a week— amounted to nearly four times her yearly salary.

Some faint, sensible part of her mind screamed at her to walk away. She knew she ought to listen.

"Soliciting sexual favors from your employees is wrong," Kate finally said, her tone ice-cold.

She hadn't realized how much Mikhail's expression had opened up until that moment. Suddenly, the vulnerability, the hope, the desire, was gone. He was back to closed inscrutability. He released his hands from behind his back and started to rise. Kate stopped him by planting her foot against his chest. The point of her heel rested directly over his heart.

He froze, looking up at her with a confused frown.

She reached into her bag, pulling out the file with the signed NDA, and dropping it on his desk. "Did I tell you you could get up?"

And then the heat was back. His face didn't shift dramatically, but the hot gleam in his eyes was unmistakable. He sank back down, hands behind his back again, and bowed his head. "I'm sorry, knyazhna."

Chapter Five

Kate drew her foot back, returning it to the floor. "I should punish you for your disgusting behavior."

His gaze flew to hers, bright and hungry, before he quickly cast it back down. "Yes, knyazhna."

A hot thrill ran down Kate's spine. She stared down at him, arms crossed. "Before this goes any further, tell me your safeword."

Mikhail shook his head, brows drawing together. "I don't have one. I don't want one."

"Well, *I* want one. So consider this a command—give me a safeword."

He gazed up at her, sullen reluctance warring with his obvious desire to continue. "Choose one for me."

Kate shrugged. "Red for stop, yellow for slow down, green for keep going. Okay?"

"Yes, alright," he huffed, clearly having no intention of using them.

"If I ask for a color, you better be prepared to answer me," she snapped.

Her tone blotted the sullenness out of his gaze. "Yes," he said. "I will."

"Alright. Give me a color then."

His lips quirked, amused but still game. "Green."

"Good boy." She let her gaze track over him, taking her time about it. "If I own you, I want to see my possession. Shirt off."

He moved with swift obedience. The muscles in his forearms flexed as he unbuttoned his shirt, sliding it off to reveal a plain white undershirt stretched over a broad chest. A silver chain with a small oval pendant circled his neck, resting against thick, black chest hair.

Kate pushed off of the desk, bending down to examine the necklace. Mikhail held stock still as she lifted the pendant. It was a saint medal, the Virgin Mary, cast in a style that looked Byzantine rather than Roman.

"Are you religious?" she asked.

He kept his gaze downcast. "No." There was a world of unsaid meaning contained in that single, curt reply. If she commanded him to explain, would he obey? She wasn't sure she wanted to find out. She wasn't sure she even wanted to know anything about what the medal meant to him. The less she knew about him, the more two-dimensional he remained, the more easily she could boss him around without the faintest qualm.

She dropped the pendant and straightened, stepping back to prop herself against the edge of the desk again. "Undershirt off," she commanded.

He reached behind himself, grabbing the back of his shirt and pulling it over his head in that way that men always did. Why was it so hot when they did that? Kate blinked, working to keep her expression unflustered.

He lowered his arms again, and suddenly a whole lot of bare skin was on display. Coarse, black hair covered his chest and ran down his abdomen in a broad swath. He was thick through the torso, dense with muscle, but not cut with gym-rat definition. His strength was evident, but not flashy. He looked like he could yoke a team of oxen to plow, or split a full cord of wood with an ax, and then use the logs to build a cabin by hand. He was easily strong enough to overpower Kate, and the fact that he'd instead knelt before her, surrendered all that strength to her, sent another hot flush chasing over her skin.

She suppressed a shiver, crossing her arms over her chest to feign nonchalance. "Take off everything. You're being punished. You'll have to earn clothing back."

He reached for his belt. It jingled as he worked it free. As he unbuttoned his trousers and pulled the zipper down, Kate recognized the flaw in her command.

"You can get off your knees to undress. Then right back down."

"Yes, knyazhna." He shifted his weight onto his ass, unfolding his legs so that he could remove his shoes.

"What are you calling me?" Kate asked, genuinely curious.

"Knyazhna. It is a royal title. For a princess."

Unexpected warmth bloomed in her chest. She hadn't expected something so sweet. She'd assumed it would mean "mistress" or "boss" or something equally cold—something that cast her as a dispassionate authority. Instead, he'd given her an honorific so sweetly feminine, it made her want to forget about punishing him.

But as he worked his trousers and tight boxer briefs down his legs, Kate immediately rejected the notion. He was as hard as a rock, thick cock straining urgently upward. He was uncut, the foreskin drawn back by his erection, but still circling the lower portion of his glans. Veins traced beneath the fine skin, starkly defined.

He stepped out of his trousers and shifted back to kneeling, hands behind his back once more. He looked up to Kate, and as her gaze met his, his cock gave an excited pulse.

Kate was at a bit of a loss. Hot, sweaty lust was tangling up her insides, but as much as she loved having this level of power over a man, she hadn't anticipated it with Mikhail. She should have. He'd as good as told her in his office that he was submissive. It was just so hard to reconcile the intimidating force of his presence with the idea of his submission. Kate had been expecting a proposal where she ostensibly had "control" in the sense that she'd be doing all the work while Mikhail laid back and received whatever pleasure she doled out. Instead, he was offering true submission, and it was screwing with her head.

"Show me how sorry you are," she finally said, trying to project an imperial air to disguise her floundering.

Mikhail didn't seem put off by the open-ended command. He brought his hands forward, bracing against the floor. His arms and shoulders spread wide as he lowered himself, the muscles in his back standing out in stark relief. He bent his head and kissed the top of her foot. Even through the thin nylon weave of Kate's stockings, his lips were soft and hot against her skin. They drifted higher, pressing to a sensitive spot on the inside of her ankle, and Kate had to suppress another aroused shiver. Christ, if the man could do this much just by pressing his lips to her foot, God knew what he was going to be like when they actually fucked.

"Forgive me, knyazhna," he breathed against her skin, lips sliding higher up her calf. "I'm sorry. Let me please you."

He rose higher, kissing the inside of her knee now. His lips parted and his tongue slipped out, wetting her skin through the stocking. This time she couldn't repress the pleased shiver. Her whole body felt too warm, her skin too tight. Her nipples were hard points. She gripped the edge of the desk with tightly clenched fingers in an effort to keep herself still.

He reached the hem of her dress, nuzzling her inner thigh. "Lift your dress for me, knyazhna. Let me taste you."

Somehow, Kate found it in herself to maintain control. "Are you giving me orders?"

"No," he breathed, kissing her inner thighs, trying to push his face beneath the hem of her dress. "Never. I want to please you."

"You want to please yourself." Kate squeezed her thighs together, closing him out. "But this is supposed to be a punishment. I don't think I should let you touch me."

"Please, knyazhna. I *need* to." His hands were on her now, cupping the backs of her calves as he pressed his face into the juncture of her thighs.

Even through her skirt and underwear, she felt the bridge of his nose nudge against her mons, putting indirect pressure on her clit. She caught a handful of hair, pulling his head back. He stared up at her, lips parted, cheeks flushed, eyes glassy with desire. The cold, stoic mask was nowhere in sight. This was the real man, stripped of his armor, weaknesses bared unflinchingly for Kate.

She tightened her hold on his hair, pulling his head back a little further, leaning in close so she could speak softly. "I think I should make you kneel in the corner, hands behind your back, and watch while I take care of myself."

Alarm and furious desire clashed in his pained expression, thick brows drawing together, forehead creased. "My tongue is better than your hand."

She laughed, delighted by his audacity. "You think *you* know how to make me come better than *I* do?"

"I know I do." His voice emerged as a growl as his hands tightened on her calves.

"Careful," she warned, giving his hair a sharp tug.

He grunted, easing back, loosening his grip. "Let me prove it."

"Hmm..." She tapped her chin with one finger, gaze wandering over his naked body—from the firmly bunched muscles of his broad shoulders, down that darkly furred chest and abdomen, to the rampant jut of his cock, the crown already glistening with pre-come. She shifted one foot forward, brushing the toe of her shoe along the underside of his shaft.

Mikhail sucked in a staggered breath, nearly doubling over at the shock of sensation. Kate pressed the toe of her shoe very delicately against the juncture where the base of his shaft and the top of his sac met. He groaned, eyes squeezing shut, hands clenching on her calves.

"*Ah,* please, knyazhna! Moya printsessa, ya vas umolyayu —let me—" Russian and English bled together into an incomprehensible language made up only of pleading sounds as something wet touched the top of Kate's foot, seeping through her stocking. She glanced down—pre-come wept in a thin strand from the tip of his cock to her foot.

"You're making a mess," she said sulkily, pressing her toe in just a bit harder.

"*Ah!* Forgive me, knyazhna. Please, let me—*fuck*. I need —pozhaluysta, moya printsessa—" He drew in a pained breath. His voice sounded even deeper in Russian. "Let me make it up to you." His whole body seemed somehow bigger, more muscular, as he strained to remain kneeling at her feet.

"Make up for what?"

"Making a mess."

"And what else?" She dug her toe in just a *bit* harder, rewarded with a choked groan.

"Propositioning you."

"That's right. Are you ashamed of yourself?"

"No."

Kate laughed out loud, unable to help herself. That was *not* the answer she was expecting. Struggling to school her features into seriousness, she ended up grinning at him as she informed him, "You should be."

"But I can't be, because now you are my printsessa."

Charming, sneaky bastard. She had to move away from sentimental talk or she'd end up cuddling him like a puppy. Apparently she was a very soft domme, but she sensed that she was not being paid for softness.

"How would you make up for your bad behavior?" she asked, drawing her foot away and releasing her grip on his hair. Indulging herself for a moment, she pet him, stroking her fingertips along his scalp where previously she'd been pulling.

He let out a gravelly sigh, leaning into her touch like an affectionate wolf. "Let me make you come with my mouth."

"Hm... I don't know. I think you might enjoy it too much." Kate wanted to find out what that mouth could do, but she was enjoying his desperation, and based on the puddle of pre-come on her foot, so was he.

"I wouldn't take my own pleasure," he promised, turning his head to kiss her thigh. "I swear. Only let me give you yours, knyazhna."

Kate gazed down at him, suddenly hit with the stark awareness that this was *Mikhail Volkov*, in a way she hadn't been before. The picture he presented was almost profane. Not because of his nakedness or his arousal, but because of what he represented—power, wealth, masculinity—and what she'd done to him. If the tech and finance bros, the "rise and grind" bootstrap-pullers, the self-declared "alphas," could see their patron saint now, they'd be stunned by the sacrilege.

Kate smiled and leaned back, bracing her hands against the desk as she parted her thighs. "Alright, then. Convince me you're sorry."

His hands slid up the backs of her calves, gripping behind her knees and pulling her legs wider apart. Kate gasped, a shock of pleasure shooting straight to her core. Her skirt slid up her thighs, revealing the tiny lace undies she'd worn in anticipation of having them seen. She hadn't imagined, though, that they'd be witnessed this close up. Mikhail buried his face between her thighs, nose nuzzling over her mons, inhaling deeply of her scent.

"*Ah,*" he breathed out, the sigh of a parched man finally getting a drink of water. "Needed this since you first touched me." His deep voice rumbled against her skin, sending gentle vibrations straight to her sensitive flesh.

Kate drew in a stuttering breath, trying to keep her composure. Mikhail nuzzled deeper, the bridge of his nose pressing the wet lace of her panties into the seam of her pussy, nudging against her clit. Kate damn near shot out of her skin at the burst of sensation. Christ, all the teasing had gotten her revved. She was already on the edge of coming.

Mikhail let out a pleasured growl at her reaction. His hands tightened behind her knees, suddenly slinging her legs up and over his shoulders, then sliding up to grip her hips. His tongue slicked out, stroking over lace and dragging around her clit.

"Jesus fuck," Kate gasped, bracing herself on her elbows as she stared down at him, legs already beginning to shake. Her heels had slipped off, hanging onto each foot by her curled toes.

One of Mikhail's hands abandoned its grip on her hip, slipping over her thigh to reach for her panties. With a firm yank, he ripped them away. Kate yelped as the elastic bit painfully into her skin, but the pain only heightened everything else she was feeling.

"You're going to pay for those," she managed to gasp.

He wasted no time with a response. His mouth was already on her slick, hot, swollen flesh, lapping up the taste of her in long, thorough strokes. A few days ago, she'd gotten a full Brazilian wax for the first time in eons, and she was suddenly intensely grateful for it. She felt his tongue *everywhere*. Her whole body was covered in goosebumps. Her pussy was covered in goosebumps. Hell, her ovaries were probably covered in goosebumps.

Mikhail ate her out like she was the one paying him. Like his life depended on it. Like giving her pleasure was the only thing keeping the world spinning. He brought her near the peak again and again, letting her get a little closer and a little closer, until her whole body was sheened with sweat, trembling all over, and her breaths were coming in desperate, keening gasps.

With a crazed snarl, she snatched his hair with one hand, tugging hard. "Enough playing," she said in a tone that was meant to be authoritative, but probably sounded a lot like begging. "Make me come before I—*ah*, fuck!—before I lose my patien—"

Her words were lost in a silent scream as Mikhail closed his lips around her clit and sucked. She fell back flat across the surface of his desk, back arching, hips rolling, as a once-in-a-lifetime orgasm roared through her. It seemed to go on forever, washing through her entire body in potent waves, rippling outward from the magic of Mikhail's tongue.

When at last the pleasure began to ebb, Mikhail softened his mouth, stroking his tongue gently over the contours of her pussy, delicately tracing her slit, her lips, her folds. Kate lay limp and stunned across the desk, vaguely aware that there was a pen and a phone jabbing her in the back.

Mikhail's mouth moved to her thighs, dragging soft little kisses. "Knyazhna?"

"Hm?" Kate pushed herself up unsteadily. Her hand slid on a sheaf of papers, but she caught herself, sitting up to gaze down at him. She had never revered his wealth or his personal power—had resented it actually, even as she worked for him. But that no longer mattered, because she might start worshipping him for his oral skills alone.

"Did I prove myself?"

There was such blatant arrogance in his tone that it immediately washed away Kate's dazed, sex-drunk weakness. She slid her thighs from his shoulders and planted one foot on his chest, shoving him backwards. He grunted as he landed on his ass, looking up at her with a mix of confusion and smugness. He was still achingly erect, and a puddle of pre-come had pooled beneath him on the floor.

"Did I do something wrong?" he asked, in a tone that implied *I know I haven't.*

"You proved your tongue is useful for one thing," Kate said archly, "but it isn't talking."

"Knyazhna," he began, a conciliatory note in his voice even as his eyes continued to gleam with self-satisfied cockiness. "I—"

"No. You know you weren't apologizing with that little demonstration." She slid off of the desk onto stockinged feet and straightened the hem of her dress as she glanced around for her shoes. "So your punishment is not over."

His cock pulsed, another little stream of pre-come oozing from the tip. "Knyazhna—"

"On your knees. Hands behind your back when I address you."

He shifted to comply, the smug gleam fading from his eyes, replaced by glazed, lust-struck vagueness. His blatant susceptibility to her control was such a pleasure, her pussy gave a little squeeze at the sight.

"If you had convinced me that you were properly sorry, I would have let you come."

A soft, pained groan sounded in his throat.

"But since you decided to put on a show instead, you lost the privilege."

"Knyazhna, please—"

"Don't interrupt me." She found her shoes and slipped one, then the other, back on. She spotted her torn panties beside the desk and decided they were a lost cause. "You're not allowed to come until the next time we meet."

Mikhail twisted towards her, reaching out desperately. "Knyazhna, please, I need to come. I need—"

"You should have thought of that beforehand." She stepped out of his reach, heading towards the door. "Maybe next time you'll serve me properly. I reward good behavior."

Halfway to the door, she paused, arrested by an antique marble chess set on a small table flanked by two chairs. Kate took a step closer, looking down. A game was in progress—white's turn. Black had already castled their king.

Kate glanced back at Mikhail. He was kneeling, his weight braced on his hands, his face a mask of torment as he watched her. The man could have anything he wanted in the world, except the one thing he wanted most right now—because she'd told him he couldn't.

Kate turned back to the chessboard and moved the white knight to g6. "Check," she said softly. "Hope your attitude's better next time."

And she left.

MIKHAIL WAS IN A HORRIFIC AGONY OF HIGHLY STOKED, unresolved arousal. And he was ecstatic about it. The temptation to relieve himself was overpowering, but even *that* pain, the struggle to resist, he savored. It was the feeling of her control, even after she was gone. And the denial, her orders, would linger with him until they next met.

She was every bit the force of nature he'd anticipated. She was more, even. Stronger, sharper, stricter. The give and take between them felt so instinctive, so right, his mind was turning to absurd ideas that he'd never entertained over a woman before. Making their arrangement permanent in some way. Giving her a place in his home so she could rule over him every minute he was away from work. Which, granted, didn't amount to many minutes—but it would be more than their current arrangement allowed for.

He already knew this was a fascination that wouldn't burn out as quickly as his past arrangements had. Those had been wholly transactional. As soon as the women were gone, he did not think of them until his libido compelled him to. But with Kate, there was an intense mutuality that had electrified him day and night since he'd met her.

He didn't know quite how to define the feeling. He didn't have much experience with softer sentiments like affection or fondness, and certainly not that most distant one —love. Raised as a ward of the state in the former Soviet Union, he'd had friends among his fellow orphans, and favorite house matrons in the orphanages and boarding schools, but all of the greatest pleasures in his life had come from the unsentimental parts of his psyche—first, from his academic talents, which brought him to the U.S. for graduate school and laid the groundwork for his career in computer engineering, then from his analytic skills as a businessman, which had brought him all the wealth, comfort, privilege, and safety that he currently enjoyed.

And that wealth and privilege had brought him to *her*. In a mere fifteen minutes, Kate Pasternak had given him the most gratifying session of power exchange that he'd yet experienced. Never mind the tameness of the acts. Never mind that he'd been denied his own release. Something fit with the two of them in a way he'd never experienced before. It was instinctive and natural and explosive and bafflingly compelling.

He'd given her an honorific he'd never used before— never *thought* to use before—but it fit her so perfectly, it had fallen from his lips without thought. She wasn't a cold, cruel mistress. Not a remote, untouchable goddess. She was his princess, yego knyazhna. She was feminine and powerful, capricious and playful, sweet and dangerous. He could still taste her on his tongue, and he wanted nothing more than to drag her back here and make her come on his face again and again and again.

He got to his feet, groaning at the heavy, tender ache in his groin. He dressed slowly, hyper-aware of the slide of the clothing over his skin, delicately maneuvering his stiff, sensitized cock back into the confines of his trousers. Walking like he'd just gotten off a horse, he went to the chessboard, intending to replace the piece Kate had moved. He'd been playing a match against himself, and he expected her "check" declaration had been nothing more than a bit of showmanship before she left him.

But when he reached the board, he found himself staring down at her move with a measure of appreciation. She'd made a valid move. And not only that, a reasonably clever one. Getting out of check would be easy, but he would waste a turn doing so. Which would allow her to take his rook with her queen on her next turn, setting up a potential checkmate in two more moves if he didn't do something about the knight on g6.

A slow grin stretched his face. Forgetting the ache of unrelieved arousal, he pulled out the nearest chair and settled in to contemplate his next few moves.

Chapter Six

Saturday morning, Kate woke to a notification on her phone. Five-thousand dollars had been deposited into her checking account. She laughed in disbelief as she stared at the screen. Mikhail had made her come so hard, he might have literally fucked her brains out, because she had completely forgotten about the money.

Before she did the sensible thing—putting it towards her remaining debts—she needed to be a little self-indulgent. She needed new black pumps before the loose heel came off on her current pair. She also desperately needed a new winter coat, and she wanted a *nice* one. She'd been scouring luxury second-hand sites, hoping to score a decent coat for a reasonable amount of money, but she hadn't yet found any that fit her taste and fell within her budget. Now she didn't have to.

Kate got dressed and made her way over to the Gold Coast. For the first time since moving to the city, she was headed to Oak Street to actually buy something instead of just staring enviously through store windows.

Four hours later, she had spent a little over two thousand

dollars on three different pairs of shoes—a beautiful pair of black T-strap heels that made her feel like a 1930s Parisian lounge singer, another beautiful pair of black d'Orsay pumps with golden spikes on the heel that made her feel like the evil bitch character in a bad action movie, and a pair of brown knee-high lace-up riding boots that made her feel like she also needed aviator's goggles and a pixie cut.

She resisted the temptation to spend another few thousand on new work clothes, instead putting just over four grand on a goose-down coat. The dove gray cashmere shell had a subtle tweed pattern that screamed *quality*. It was so beautifully constructed, it was hard to believe it was such a well-insulated coat. It looked too pretty to be so functional. She'd never owned something so perfect in all her life. She'd never been the sort of person who had nice things. She'd never felt like the sort of person who deserved nice things.

Arguably, nobody *deserved* a four thousand dollar coat. But Kate had one now, and as she stroked her hand over the wool, she was overwhelmed by a strange feeling. Her throat and chest tightened. Her hand shook. The feeling reminded her a little bit of what it'd been like when she'd first befriended Anna five years ago—when she'd realized she'd somehow gained the affection of somebody so much better than her. If there was a name for that feeling, Kate didn't know what it was. Pride and fear and comfort and shame all rolled into one confusing jumble.

She had just gotten back to her apartment, still tangled in that strange melancholy, when her phone rang. She pulled it out and groaned. It was her mom. Just what she needed for her current mood. Her mom had gotten sober a few years ago, and she was generally okay to talk to, but Kate had never figured out how to get past the resentment of her childhood.

She was glad her mom was healthier now, but where the fuck had that willpower been when she'd had two little kids depending on her?

Kate let the phone ring a few times, slumped against her front door as she stared at the screen, deliberating. Finally, she sighed and answered it. "Hey, mom."

"Hey, Trina."

Kate cringed. She hated that name. It's what everyone back home called her. It was her trailer park name. Her white trash name. As soon as she'd gotten the fuck out of Whispering Pines Trailer Court, on her first day of classes at the technical college—a new world where nobody knew who she was or where she'd come from—she'd introduced herself as Kate, and she'd never looked back.

"Katrina? Baby?"

Kate had been quiet too long. "Sorry, Mom. I spaced out. How're you doing?" She cringed again. The northern Wisconsin accent had come out hard on that last bit. Talking to her family always resurrected it.

"Well, I'm alright. But Angel's in a tough spot."

Kate's sister, Angela, was her identical twin, but no two people had ever been less alike. Kate valued self-control beyond anything else, while Angel was impulsive, messy, and loud. Kate had left their shitty hometown at the first opportunity, Angel had stayed. After growing up under the erratic care of two alcoholics, Kate was a teetotaler in every regard. Meanwhile, Angel had multiple drunk-and-disorderlies and several possession charges to her name. Kate had avoided so much as breathing the same air with any man who could drag her down, while Angel was stuck with two different losers who owed her thousands in unpaid child support. Which was less of an issue now that CPS had taken Angel's kids away and placed them with Auntie Deb, the only halfway decent person in their entire family.

Kate sighed. "Don't tell me she got kicked out of another club." Angel worked sporadically as a stripper, but she'd already been banned from clubs in Green Bay, Appleton, and Milwaukee for fighting the other girls and bringing in drugs.

"Well..."

"Mom."

"Well, it's not her fault when they gang up on her and she defends herself!" Mom's voice was too deep and raspy for her age, but that was what thirty-some years of a pack-a-day habit and two handles a week did to the vocal cords.

"Yeah. I'm sure that's what happened." It was always everyone else who was the problem, never Angel.

"She's your sister," Mom huffed. "You have to stand by your family."

Kate said nothing.

"*Anyway*," Mom went on, "they set her bail at five thousand and we only need seven hundred more to get her out."

"Wow, that sucks. What're you going to do?" Kate asked blandly.

"Well, you've got a little cash, dontcha? Big city girl."

"Not a red cent," she lied. Had Mom called before she'd met Mikhail Volkov, she'd be able to tell the truth without a single qualm. She didn't feel any qualms now, but she recognized that normal people probably would have.

"Deb says you're making seventy-k a year."

"Aunt Deb's wrong." She made slightly less than that. "And even if I did, seventy thousand doesn't get you far in Chicago."

"Gets you far enough, apparently. I don't see you struggling like your sister does."

"That's because I don't do the kind of dumb-ass shit Angel's always doing," Kate snapped. "For example, I never got kicked out of a job and arrested because I kept attacking my fucking coworkers!"

"So, you're perfect?" Mom asked heatedly. "You're just going to abandon her? Just leave her to suffer?"

"Yeah, that's exactly what I'm going to do," Kate said furiously. "I'm not setting myself on fire to keep Angel warm."

"Get over yourself," Mom groused. "She'll pay you back."

Kate laughed and laughed and laughed. And then she laughed some more. "Good one."

"Well, then *I'll* pay you back."

"No. It's not happening."

"When did you become such a bitch?"

"A long time ago. Bye, Mom." Kate hung up and flung her phone away. It landed on her sofa with a heavy *thwack*. She exhaled a long, slow, deep-bellied sigh that slowly turned into a growl and then into a primal scream. She pressed her hands over her mouth muffling the noise so her neighbors wouldn't hear. She squeezed her eyes shut and screamed into her palm until her throat ached and her temples throbbed.

When she pulled her hands away from her mouth, her breath came in ragged gasps. She tilted her head back against the door, staring up at the ceiling while she waited for her blood pressure to drop and her breathing to even out.

You're not like them, she reminded herself. She'd left that world behind. She hadn't spoken to Angel in over a year— hadn't seen her face in more than three. If she had her way, she'd never see Angel again. Angel was like a Dickensian ghost of what might have been—if Kate had never left Whispering Pines, if she hadn't gotten that abortion when she was seventeen, if she hadn't listened to her high school math teacher's urging to apply to college, if she'd missed any number of the diverging paths in her past that led her to where she was today. She couldn't bear that idea.

She pushed Angel out of her mind. A line of pain was cutting across her curled fingers on one hand, and when she looked down, she saw the shopping bag full of expensive shoe boxes, still clutched in her white-knuckled fist. The shoes were a sudden balm to her frazzled nerves. She knew it was materialistic and shallow, but having nice *things* reminded her of who she wasn't anymore. Who she would never be.

She went to her bedroom and sat on the bed, slowly unboxing each pair of shoes and admiring them like they were Christmas presents she'd just opened. She wasn't totally sure what that feeling was like. Dad had never remembered Christmas. And while Mom usually had, the gifts had always been random junk that she'd clearly bought at the last second from Big Lots. But Kate imagined kids with competent parents probably felt this warm, secure, comfortable feeling when they unwrapped the Barbies and Nerf guns they'd actually wanted.

This is unhealthy, she thought as she stared at her new shoes with glowing contentment. *But I don't care.*

On Monday Kate walked into the Domovoy building with a nervous edge of anticipation. *He* was here. The man who owned this company. The man who'd knelt at her feet and begged to eat her pussy. The very one who'd paid her five grand after she'd left him hard and unsatisfied. The five-hundred-dollar shoes on her feet, clicking briskly over the terrazzo tiles of the building's lobby, had been bought with that money. The gorgeous coat currently keeping her warm had been, too. She was dressed top to bottom in the evidence of their arrangement.

She went through security and rode the elevator up to her work floor, surrounded by people who had no idea of the filthy things she'd done to their boss. Shame and superiority mingled in equal measure, filling her with jittery energy. She pressed her lips together, fighting a crazed smile.

When she reached her floor, she walked to her desk on high alert, scanning the rows of cubicles for the sight of a dark-haired, grim-faced Russian in an impeccable suit. She knew she wasn't going to see him. And yet, she couldn't help but look. When she reached her desk, she hung up her beautiful new coat on the wall of her cubicle, petting it fondly, and then sank into her desk chair.

Within the hour, she was absorbed by her work, all thoughts of Mikhail Volkov shunted to the back of her mind. Until two weeks ago, she'd never even seen him in person, despite having worked for Domovoy for three years. The odds of her running into him again were essentially nil. A few hours later, she'd almost entirely forgotten about him.

Later that afternoon, she was leaving a meeting on the ninth floor, taking the roundabout way back to her own department when she spotted a tall, broad, be-suited figure approaching from the opposite end of the long hallway. She recognized Mikhail immediately. His size, his stride, his hardened expression.

He seemed like a different person. He was dressed in a dark blue suit that probably cost more than her car. His expression was cold, hard, remote. He carried himself with a natural aura of command and control. Kate could hardly believe she'd had him on his knees.

He glanced up from his phone, gaze flicking over to her as they strode towards one another. Something hot and wicked flashed in his eyes, even as his face remained utterly stoic.

"Ms. Pasternak," he greeted her in that deep voice, rolling the r in her name and shifting the sounds of the vowels. She loved the way he pronounced her name. Would it be weird if she started making everyone pronounce it that way? Probably.

"Mr. Volkov," she greeted him in return, a hot flush creeping up her neck. The image of him dropping to his knees in that beautiful suit, doing whatever she commanded of him, filled her mind.

But the man stopping in front of her wasn't *that* man. Not right now. His gaze ran up and down her body, but there was none of the eager servant in his eyes. Instead, she found herself caught in the sights of a wolf—a hungry wolf.

"Nice shoes," he said, the corner of his lip curling ever-so-slightly upward.

She resisted the urge to glance down at her brand-new heels. She'd tamed that wolf, she reminded herself, tilting her chin up to glare at him. He was challenging her with that smile, with his over-familiarity. She wouldn't have expected the dynamic of their arrangement to extend beyond the bounds of their private meet-ups, but that belligerent gaze declared otherwise.

"Thank you," she replied briskly. "They're great for stepping on throats."

His gaze darkened. "Only *one* throat."

Kate couldn't help a smirk. Before she could speak, Mikhail's big body was crowding her back against the wall. He braced one hand on the wall next to her head, caging her in as he glared down at her.

"Only one," he repeated in a low growl.

Kate didn't appreciate being intimidated, or the implication in his demand. She grabbed his tie and jerked, pulling his face close to hers. "Are you questioning my integrity?" she asked in a dangerously soft voice.

Mikhail's hard expression slackened a touch, his dark gaze losing some of its focus. He swallowed, taking a moment to answer her. "No," he finally said.

Kate adjusted her grip on the tie, twisting so that it tightened around his throat. "Are you sure about that?"

Neither one of them moved, but the nature of their stances had abruptly changed. Mikhail wasn't caging her in—he was the one who was trapped. He wasn't looming over her, but stooping to accommodate her height. The hand on the wall beside her head was no longer a threatening blockade to Kate, but a necessary point of balance for Mikhail.

"I'm sure, knyazhna," he whispered.

Kate twisted his tie just a little tighter. "Good." She released him, pushing against his chest. He ceded immediately, backing up a step. Kate smoothed a hand over her hair, making sure the wall hadn't mussed it. Mikhail was collecting himself as well, gaze darting up and down the hall as he smoothed his shirt back down.

"Straighten your tie," Kate said.

He did so. "Visit me tonight," he said quietly, big fingers sliding along his collar to fix the fold.

Kate considered him. "Are you that eager to be punished?"

He winced faintly. "I would rather please you."

"Maybe it pleases me to punish you."

The heat in his eyes shone brighter. He leaned closer to her, his voice pitched low. "Then I—"

The sound of approaching footsteps echoed from the adjacent corridor. Kate and Mikhail flinched away from each other. He immediately strode past her, in the direction he'd been headed before. Kate started to follow him, then remembered she'd been headed in the opposite direction. Cursing herself for an idiot, she made an embarrassing U-turn, expensive new shoes clicking a frantic staccato over the floor as she hurried away.

"Oh, Mr. Volkov!" a young man's voice greeted him brightly. "I was going to wait until the meeting this afternoon, but since I ran into you..."

Kate rounded the next corner, losing the rest of whatever the man was saying. Her heart was hammering, her breath coming too quickly, too shallowly. It had been a close call, but that wasn't what had her pulse pounding. It was the look in his eyes while she'd choked him with his own tie. The deep purr of his voice when he'd started to whisper something wicked to her. She pressed the backs of her hands to her heated cheeks, fighting a ridiculous grin.

Just as she reached the elevators, her phone buzzed. She fished it out of her pocket and glanced at the screen.

My driver will pick you up at seven.

Chapter Seven

Kate's nerves were no calmer this time than they'd been the first time she'd arrived at Mikhail's house. David Marx, the household manager, greeted her again and led her through the side entry.

"Mr. Volkov is in his office, but he said to show you up right away," he explained as he took her coat and bag.

She followed him through the massive house, treading the same path they'd followed last time. The door to Mikhail's office was ajar and his voice could be heard, speaking in a low rumble. Kate hesitated at the doorway, uncertain if she should walk in on what could be a confidential business conversation. But David gestured her in, so in she went.

Mikhail sat at his desk, still wearing his suit from work, brow furrowed as he continued speaking to the video conference on his laptop. He wasn't speaking English, Kate realized. It wasn't Russian either. It sounded like Mandarin, maybe, though she didn't know a single word in the language, so she couldn't really be sure.

Mikhail glanced up when Kate appeared in the doorway. His expression didn't change at all, but something about him *intensified* at the sight of her. He said something brief to the other parties in the video conference, tapped a few keys, and closed his laptop, turning his full attention to Kate.

"Thank you, David," Mikhail said, dark gaze burning into Kate. "Enjoy your night."

David nodded. "You as well, sir. And you, Ms. Pasternak." He turned and left.

Kate crossed her arms, leaning against the door frame, and gazed back at Mikhail. It was hard to fathom that she was supposed to be the one in control here. He was such an intense man. He didn't have to speak or posture or threaten. His mere presence exuded its own force. It was up to Kate to leash all that and bring him to heel.

"I sent all the household staff home," he said. "We're alone."

Biting back a smile, she sauntered towards his desk, coming around to sit on the edge, just beside his laptop. "Then why are you dressed? I didn't tell you you'd earned your clothing back."

He pushed back from his desk and stood up, immediately shrugging out of his suit jacket. He loosened his tie and dropped it on the desk, then deftly unbuttoned his shirt. Piece by piece, he stripped away his veneer of civility until he was bare before her.

"On your knees," she commanded.

He sank down, hands clasped behind his back. His big thighs were spread wide, his cock twitching to attention.

"Have you touched yourself since last time?"

"No, knyazhna."

"Not even a little?"

"No," he insisted vehemently.

"Good. Then we're going to have a do-over. If you can prove that you've learned your lesson, maybe you'll get a reward."

"Yes, knyazhna."

"Good. Now, show me how sorry you are."

The pain of denial must have left a significant impression on him. He began at her feet, kissing and caressing his way upwards, worshipping every inch of her with slow, thorough dedication. His mouth and hands set every nerve of hers alight, sent delicious sensation shimmering over her whole body. When he pulled her panties away, he was careful not to rip them. When he buried his face between her thighs, licking and sucking and devouring, he did so with the same artful passion as before.

But this time, after she came, there was no smug arrogance. There was only the glassy-eyed, flushed look of a desperately horny man, deeply in need of relief.

"What do you have to say for yourself?" Kate demanded breathlessly, her whole body still buzzy and light from post-orgasm endorphins.

"Thank you for letting me serve you," Mikhail said thickly, his voice husky with arousal and deprivation.

"Alright," she conceded. "You're back in my good graces. Stand up."

He did so unsteadily, bracing one hand on the edge of the desk. Kate leaned forward, taking his cock in hand and stroking him hard.

"You haven't earned the right to come inside me," she told him over the sound of his labored breathing. "But you are allowed to come." She stroked harder, gripped him tighter. "Come for me, pet."

He groaned, bowing over, held upright only by the hand gripping the desk. His cock pulsed in her grasp, and he shouted incoherently as he came, painting stripes of white across Kate's thighs. It seemed to go on forever, making him shake and groan, and draining an impressive amount of semen from him.

"There we go," Kate soothed, stroking him through the last few pulses. "That's better, hm?"

He laughed weakly. "Thank you, knyazhna."

When she released him, he remained bent over, hauling in rough breaths. After a moment, he managed to straighten up.

"I'll get something to clean up." He left the office.

Kate listened to the sound of his footsteps in the hall, the opening of another door, the sound of running water. A moment later, he reappeared with a wet washcloth.

Kate reached for it, but Mikhail pulled it away. "*I will do it.*"

She glared at him. "Is that how you speak to me?"

"Please," he amended quickly. "Let me serve you."

"Fine." She leaned back on the desk, affecting an air of indolence as Mikhail stepped between her spread thighs. Gently, he stroked the warm wet cloth between her thighs and then over them, swiping away the slick, shining evidence of both of their pleasure. When he was done, he brought the cloth to his face and inhaled. His heavy-lidded gaze met hers.

Kate stared at him as her whole body flushed with reawakened arousal. She reached out suddenly, catching Mikhail by the jaw, pulling his face close to hers. "That was incredibly hot."

He smiled, transforming the harshness of his features into something almost boyish. The urge to kiss him overwhelmed her and she couldn't resist it. She leaned in, softly touching her lips to his. When she pulled back, the smile had dropped from his face, and he stared at her with an expression of mild confusion.

Of course he did. They weren't lovers. This wasn't a sweet, post-coital-kisses kind of relationship. She was a paid contractor.

Mortified, Kate released his jaw and turned away. Getting to her feet, she straightened her skirt down her thighs, trying to regain some semblance of dignity.

"Where's the bathroom?" she asked.

He pushed himself up to sit, naked and sticky with come and sweat. "Go left down the hall, it's the second door on the right."

"Thank you." She started to walk away, then turned back. Despite the flush in her cheeks, she adopted a haughty demeanor. "I'm sure you can find another bathroom in this labyrinth of a house. Go clean yourself up."

A hint of a smile tugged at one corner of his mouth. "Yes, knyazhna."

When Kate returned to Mikhail's office, he was already back. He was in the process of stepping into his pants, pulling them up his long legs. The harsh lines of his stoic face and the sturdy, hairy expanse of his broad chest seemed at odds with the elegantly cut trousers. Still flushed from exertion, a light sheen of sweat covering his skin, he looked like a barbarian who'd murdered an aristocrat and stolen his fine clothes.

Dressing himself was a pretty clear sign that he was done, and that Kate was free to go. After all, she hadn't given him his rights to clothing back yet, and he didn't have a belligerent expression on his face to suggest that this was an attempt to provoke her. The game was over for now.

"How do I get home if you gave all your staff the night off?" She asked, crossing the office to retrieve her shoes.

"My driver is on call tonight. I can have him here in a few minutes."

"Okay." She walked over to the small table with the chess set, using it to balance as she slipped one shoe on, then the other. Briefly, she glanced at the board, then away. A second later, she glanced back. Mikhail had responded to her move on Saturday, getting his king out of check. Everything else was as it had been. She looked over at him and found him watching her intently.

"What's your next move, knyazhna?"

Unable to resist, she stepped closer to the board, examining the layout more carefully than she had last time. If she took his queenside rook with her queen, he'd be left with a knight and bishop standing in the way of a checkmate. Three moves. *But...* he was only two moves away from capturing her knight with his own lurking knight—leaving him perfectly set up to capture her queen if she'd taken the bishop by then. Either way, unless he was completely incompetent, he'd move his knight to protect that space.

She frowned, pinching her lower lip as her gaze traced over the board, playing out potential moves in her head. Finally, smiling to herself, she slid her queen pawn to d4, opening up a lane for her queenside bishop to defend the knight on h6. It wasn't a perfect solution—Mikhail would probably decide it was worth losing his own knight to capture hers, but still, the threat would make him think twice.

She slid a sneaky glance at him. His attention was riveted

on the board, his eyes dancing from piece to piece. Trying to find a solution that allowed him to save his own knight while getting rid of the threat hers posed. After a moment, he moved his knight in a different direction than Kate had expected. She stared at the board, trying to rationalize the move. She couldn't see anything. Was he just screwing with her?

But then she caught it—in two more moves, that knight would have two spots near her king blocked off, and if Kate didn't do anything about the bishop hanging out mid-board, he could slide that little fucker in for a checkmate.

Sometimes her aggressive play bit her in the ass—she was great at setting up attacks, but she often forgot to pay attention to defense. Luckily she'd caught it this time. Forced to abandon the set-up against his king, she slid her queen across the board to threaten both his knight and bishop at once.

Mikhail let out a little breath that sounded nearly like a laugh. He drew out the chair on the black side of the board and sank into it, using his foot to push out the other chair, gesturing distractedly for Kate to sit. Engrossed by the game, she sank into the seat, resting her elbows on the edge of the table and her chin on her folded hands. Across from her, Mikhail sat with his arms crossed over his bare chest, staring down at the board with total absorption. Finally, he moved his rook pawn forward.

The game progressed in total silence, except for annoyed huffs from Kate when Mikhail captured her rook and both bishops, and an appreciative chuckle from Mikhail when Kate took his queen. As more and more pieces left the board, their moves slowed, each taking careful stock of the board before they reacted. But in the end, just as Kate was trying to form a fork with her knight and rook, Mikhail started harrying her king. She was forced to dance her king around the board until, at last, she was out of options.

"Checkmate," Mikhail said softly, sliding his rook into place.

Kate took a second to acknowledge the wound to her pride, drawing in a slow breath and letting it out in a gusty sigh. She looked up, extending her hand across the board. "Good game."

Mikhail shook her hand. "Yes. It was. Humor me with another?"

She glanced at the window. "It's getting late." She tried to pull her hand away, but he tightened his grip.

"Please, knyazhna."

She was apparently a terrible domme, because she found his pushiness weirdly endearing. She was like the opposite of a brat tamer. She was a brat enabler.

"Alright, fine, just give me my hand back."

He flashed her a crooked smile as he released her, then immediately began setting the board up again.

Their next game was just as tense as the first, and for a while, Kate was certain of her victory. But then Mikhail ripped the rug out from under her again with a sneaky fork she hadn't been paying attention to because she'd assumed he was trying promote the pawn.

"Damn," she muttered sullenly, recognizing the checkmate two moves before it was complete. She flicked her king over.

"You're very good," Mikhail said, surveying her appreciatively.

"Not as good as you."

He smiled faintly, but there was a bitter edge to it. "I was professionally trained."

Kate's brows rose. "When?"

"When I was a child. Russia takes chess very seriously." A brief flicker of distaste crossed his face. Apparently not in the mood to elaborate, he asked, "How did you learn to play?"

"One of my dad's girlfriends taught me."

Lisa had been a bit of a train wreck, but she'd been nice to Kate. She was loud and brassy in a way that Kate, a nervous, watchful kid, had found awe-inspiring. Lisa had loved games—in addition to chess, she'd taught Kate how to play backgammon, cribbage, sheepshead, euchre, and liar's dice. Though kind, she'd been an erratic presence. She'd often disappeared for weeks at a time, was always out of work, had lost custody of her own kids, and, in hindsight, the pills she'd always been popping "for her back" had probably been an illegal opioid addiction. Kate had caught her stealing out of Dad's wallet multiple times, but she never told Dad, because she hadn't wanted him to break up with Lisa.

"*One* of his girlfriends?" Mikhail asked mildly.

Kate kept her expression perfectly blank, betraying none of the mortified shame she felt for her shitty upbringing. Lots of people had parents who weren't married to each other, Kate reminded herself. Not as many people had dads who were too busy getting drunk and chasing tail to make sure their kids had dinner, but Mikhail had no way of knowing that was the case as long as Kate didn't say anything about it.

"Yeah. He and my mom were never married. He had a few different girlfriends when I was growing up." *A few* was an understatement. Dad must've been charming as hell at the bar, because he was never single for long. Despite that, he'd driven women off just as fast he'd reeled them in.

She glanced over at Mikhail, taking in his reaction. Even

bare-chested, hair mussed, five-o'clock shadow coming in strong, he looked sturdy and competent and self-possessed. She knew his rags-to-riches story—or, at least the gist of it—but it was hard to believe he'd ever been anything but wealthy and powerful. His parents must have been the sort to appear in Soviet propaganda art. A square-jawed ironworker father and a wholesome, wheat-harvesting mother. People of humble means, but strong in spirit. Good parents who, poor or not, did everything they could for their children to succeed—who made sure their kids had clean clothes and that they took regular baths and that their hair was properly brushed every day.

At that last thought, Kate instinctively ran her fingers through her hair, paying special attention to the nape of her neck. A little mussed, but no mats. She realized Mikhail was watching her, a contemplative look on his face, and she dropped her hand, embarrassed.

He didn't know, she assured herself. Women checked their hair all the time. It was normal. There was no way for him to know that for several years, she'd been the stinky kid at school. That she'd only learned how to bathe herself properly by looking up instructions on the internet at the school library when she was in sixth grade. That she'd had to have her head shaved twice as a kid because the mats had become too severe to comb out.

"What are you thinking, knyazhna?" Mikhail asked quietly. The deep rumble of his voice, softly accented, was oddly soothing.

"You should do ASMR videos."

"What?"

A hot flush crept up her neck. She'd blurted that out without thinking. "You have a nice voice," she clarified, staring at the chessboard with excessive focus as she nudged the white pieces back to their proper places.

A beat of silence, followed by a soft chuckle. "I'll keep it in mind for a backup career."

His amusement at the very idea was a stark reminder, snapping her back into reality like a bucket of cold water turned over her head. For a while there, she'd forgotten who they were, what this was. Straightening, she got up from her chair. Mikhail's brow furrowed as he watched her.

She couldn't leave like a guest, because she wasn't one—she was the help. But she also couldn't ask to be dismissed, because deference was the exact opposite of what he was paying her for.

"It's late," she said. "I should go."

He searched her face for a moment, his expression utterly unreadable. Finally, he stood. "I'll call the driver."

———

When Kate was gone, Mikhail returned to his office and sat down at the chessboard again. He stared at the perfectly arranged pieces. After a moment, he started replaying the last game against Kate.

Not to study the gameplay. Not to develop better strategy. Just to remember. To bask in the echo of a strange warmth—a warmth that faded as soon as she was gone.

Chapter Eight

The next few days passed, and Kate saw neither hide nor hair of Mikhail. He didn't contact her. She eventually found out that he'd been in D.C., testifying to the Congressional Cybersecurity Caucus about data encryption and blockchain technology, because she saw it on the news. It hurt a little bit when she realized he hadn't told her about it. It shouldn't hurt. Logically, she knew what this was. It wasn't a real relationship. But she'd never fucked anyone without some sort of emotional commitment before, and her brain was having trouble parsing the difference.

On Thursday, she was granted a distraction in the form of her new roommate moving in. When Kate got home from work, Anna, Jason, and Naomi were already there, hauling boxes up to the fourth-floor walkup.

"Kate, you're here!" Anna wrapped her in a quick hug. "Naomi's in the bedroom, getting her things unpacked."

Kate walked over, pausing in the doorway to give her new roommate a discreet once-over. She was decidedly *not* what Kate was expecting from one of Anna's friends. Her long, thick hair was bleached peroxide white, with dark roots and thick Betty Page bangs. She had a pointed silver hoop dangling from her septum, another silver hoop circling the center of her bottom lip, and a whole cutlery drawer worth of silver hanging off her ears.

She looked like a goth Barbie, wearing a fitted black turtleneck, a black plaid skirt, and black platform mary-janes over lace-patterned black tights. She'd pushed her sleeves up to her elbows while she worked to unpack her things, revealing forearms covered in intricate black tattoos. One arm was wrapped in a beautiful cascade of realistic wildflowers, with a delicate snake twined throughout them. Its head rested on the top of her hand, eyes glittering as its forked tongue flickered out. The other forearm was inked with an elaborate interplay of Chantilly lace, faceted jewels, butterfly wings, and beaded chains. Feminine and delicate, the design ended just below her wrist with a lacy point. Kate assumed, based on the rest of her aesthetic, that there was plenty more ink hidden under her clothing.

"Hi, Naomi," Kate said, interrupting her own staring.

Naomi looked up, a heap of thick, spiral-bound sketchpads clutched to her chest. "Oh! You're Kate! Hi." Despite her bold appearance, her voice was soft and shy, just as it had sounded when they'd spoken on the phone a few weeks ago.

"Do you draw?" Kate asked, nodding to the sketchpads. She knew part of the reason Naomi had moved to Chicago was to finish an art degree.

"Oh, uh..." Naomi dropped them back into the box she'd just lifted them from and flipped the box flaps shut before she stood up. Her cheeks were flushed, her expression guarded. "Not really."

Recognizing that she didn't want to discuss it, Kate

changed topics. "How did moving in go? Sorry I couldn't be here earlier."

Naomi waved that off, weaving her way through the boxes to reach Kate. "You had to work, and I had plenty of help from Jason and Anna. Everything went smoothly." She held out her hand. "Anyway, it's nice to finally meet you in person."

Kate shook her hand, gaze tracing over tattooed flowers before lifting to that silver-studded face. Naomi's features were soft and sweet, with big, brown eyes emphasized by crisp black liner, and a delicate spray of freckles across her cheeks and nose. She was nearly as tall as Kate—which was tall for a woman, around five-nine or so—and much curvier, but Naomi radiated delicacy and reserve, while Kate had spent years purposely cultivating a Don't Fuck With Me aura.

"Well, welcome," Kate said, gesturing grandly at the small apartment. "I'm glad to have you. My last roommate was a complete flake, but Anna says you're solid, and she's never wrong."

Naomi flushed faintly. "I'll try to be."

Anna appeared at Kate's shoulder. "You guys want to get dinner?" She glanced back at Jason, who was carefully settling a box on the kitchen island. "That really good Greek place is two blocks from here."

"Let me buy dinner for you guys," Naomi said quickly. "It's the least I can do after all your help."

"You don't have to—" Anna started.

"No," Jason said bluntly. "I've got it."

"That's not how it works," Naomi objected. "I'm the one moving. I'm supposed to—"

"Text me everybody's orders," Jason said to Anna as he

threw his coat on. He looked back to Naomi. "You've got enough on your plate," he said, more gently than he'd spoken before.

That. That right there was why Kate's jealousy hadn't lasted long in the face of Anna's new relationship and—very fast—engagement. Jason was intimidating and hard to talk to, but at his core, he was a caretaker, just like Anna. He was good enough for her, which Kate hadn't initially thought possible. She was tempted to hug him, but he wasn't the sort of person who shared affection easily. Instead, she adopted the opposite tack, which was to accept his caretaking with no argument or fanfare.

"I want a gyro and two baklava!" she shouted after him as he disappeared out the front door.

"Text it to me!" he shouted back, heavy bootsteps pounding down the stairwell.

"Naomi, what do you like?" Anna asked, pulling out her phone.

"Seriously, that's so nice, but you guys have already done so much. I really don't need—"

"If you don't make a choice, he'll just get you one of everything," Anna said.

Kate gave Naomi a small nod, confirming Anna's words.

"Fine," Naomi grumbled. "A gyro sounds good."

"You should get baklava, too," Kate added.

"I don't need it."

"Gyro...and...baklava..." Anna muttered as she typed.

Naomi sighed, hiding a smile as she turned her attention to the box on the island. "Thank you," she murmured quietly to Anna.

. . .

A FEW HOURS LATER, ANNA AND JASON HAD MADE THEIR departures, and it was just Kate and Naomi in the apartment. Naomi hadn't had a whole lot to move in. Aside from a bed frame, mattress, and dresser, she'd only had a few boxes of clothing, toiletries, and some kitchen items. They were all put away, Naomi was basically settled in, and now they were left with the awkward dance of figuring out just how social they intended to be with each other.

"So... I'm going to watch TV," Kate ventured. "Do you mind if I put on *Stupid Cupid?*" It was a ridiculous reality show that Anna had gotten Kate addicted to—a bunch of insanely hot single people locked in a mansion together, trying to solve elaborate, escape-room-style riddles to win prizes—the prizes being luxurious, expensive dates, like a weekend in a tropical villa with only one bed, or a spa retreat where the winners had to give each other sensual massages.

"Oh my god," Naomi breathed, eyes going wide. "I love that show. Yes!" She plopped onto the couch next to Kate.

And just like that, the initial awkwardness was overcome.

Chapter Nine

The next day at work, Kate got a calendar alert from somebody named Sarah Engels, tagging her for a spur-of-the-moment meeting in one of the conference rooms up on the executive floor later that afternoon. She wasn't sure who Sarah Engels was, and suspected she'd been roped in for another one of those "we support women" bullshit developmental meetings that HR was always hosting, that never accomplished anything or went anywhere. It was just lip service to make it look like the company actually cared about equality or whatever.

If they cared about equality, maybe they could *actually* hire more women to leadership positions instead of badgering them into "managerial track" development programs that amounted to a bunch of unpaid labor and nothing to show for it. Maybe they should've promoted Kate to the department head position she'd applied for six months ago, instead of hiring some dumb kid straight out of college on the grounds that he had a bachelor's degree and she didn't. Like her decade of experience was nothing compared to two extra years of college classes and a big name internship.

Stop, she chided herself mentally. If she got her temper worked up before the stupid meeting even started, she'd end up getting into an argument. Last time she'd demanded to know how many of the program participants statistically went on to hold managerial positions at Domovoy. The presenter had weaseled out of answering with vague reassurances about "upward trends" and "positive outcomes." Unsatisfied, Kate had pressed for hard numbers, flustering the presenter, until one of the HR managers had stepped in and told everyone to hold their questions for the end. (Guess who didn't get called on when question time rolled around.)

Ten minutes before the appointed meeting, Kate suppressed a sigh and locked her computer. She took the stairs instead of the elevator so that she wouldn't be trapped in there with any of the HR people. They were too friendly, in a meaningless small talk kind of way. It made Kate feel irrationally annoyed.

When she reached the conference room, the lights were off and the hallway was empty. She stepped inside hesitantly, wondering if she'd gotten the room wrong. The drapes had been pulled over the windows, making the room so utterly dark that Kate couldn't see a thing. While her eyes adjusted, she felt along the wall for the light switches.

"Don't." A deep voice, a Slavic accent.

"Mikhail?"

"If you turn the lights on, you'll give our hiding spot away."

Kate bit her lip, trying to keep calm despite the frisson of excitement running up her spine. "A conference room is a terrible hiding spot." Her eyes slowly adjusted to the dark.

Mikhail was a pitch-black silhouette standing in front of the curtained windows.

"Not if the room is blocked out on the calendar and the door is locked."

Kate smiled ruefully. Taking the hint, she quietly closed the door and clicked the lock into place. The sound seemed to echo through the conference room, loosening something inside Kate's chest. She turned back to face him and swallowed a gasp. He'd crossed the room silently, standing just in front of her now. His face looked even harsher in the low light, all shadowed angles and hard lines.

Attempting to keep her cool, Kate lifted her chin, expression remote. "Who's Sarah Engels? Does she know you're using her account to set up fake meetings?"

"Sarah's my personal assistant. She'd let me use her account to commit high treason if I wanted."

"Careful, Russki. I could be a government mole."

Mikhail gave her one of his rare smiles. Her eyes had adjusted enough to the dark that she could see the details— the way his eyes creased at the corners, the slight crookedness of his canine teeth, the bristle of his five o'clock shadow coming in strong. "I'm too rich for consequences."

Well, if that wasn't a mood-killer, Kate didn't know what was. She wasn't sure how to reconcile wanting the money he was paying her while simultaneously resenting how much of it he had when too many people had too little.

Was she a hypocrite?

Nah, she thought with cynical amusement. *I'm just redistributing his wealth.*

She crossed her arms, gazing up at him with detached calm. "What was so important that you had to lure me here under false pretenses?"

"I want more," he said, stepping closer.

She held her ground, refusing to let him corral her backwards. He wanted to trap her against the wall again—he was trying to provoke her into putting him in his place. "More what?"

He made an impatient sound, half growl and half sigh, as he loomed over her, close enough to kiss, if he'd only bend down. Not that she'd do it. She'd learned her lesson with that one. The embarrassment of doing it a second time might actually kill her.

"I want your control all the time. Whenever you want it —anything you want. Any time of day."

Kate's brows rose. "Anything?"

"Yes."

"So, if I told you how to dress in the morning?"

"Yes," he said thickly, pressing even closer to her.

"And if I said you have to get permission from me before you eat anything?"

"Yes."

"What if I wanted you to send me compromising photos and videos of yourself?"

"*Fuck*," he groaned. "Yes."

"What if I wanted to lock your cock in a chastity cage?"

He winced, looking a little unnerved at that one. "If you ordered it, I would do it," he said with obvious reluctance.

Was there anything he wouldn't do? Everyone had limits. If he wouldn't disclose his, Kate would find them. "And if I told you to step down as CEO?"

Mikhail stiffened, the hunger clearing from his expression. "Alright, knyazhna, not *anything*. Nothing that would endanger my position or my company."

She smiled wryly, tilting her head to meet his chagrined

gaze. "I figured as much." Nothing that would threaten his wealth or power—that was his limit. She could've pointed out the irony, but instead, she said, "You want more from me? Then I want more money."

As soon as the words slipped out of her mouth, Kate regretted them. It'd sounded good in her head—the pushy, spoiled princess, demanding more from her loyal slave. But in the cold face of reality, it suddenly occurred to her that Mikhail might say no.

But he didn't. "I'll give you a card with an unlimited line of credit."

She didn't respond immediately, not certain she'd heard him correctly. "*Unlimited?* Come on."

"I'm completely serious."

He clearly meant it, and yet, Kate couldn't wrap her head around it. "You're just going to hand over a credit card with no limits? What if I bankrupted you?"

Mikhail barked with laughter, eyes crinkling again as he grinned at her. "I am a *very* wealthy man, knyazhna."

Kate's pride took his words as a challenge. She raised an eyebrow, fixing him with a haughty glare. "You don't think I could spend all your money?"

The mirth faded from Mikhail's eyes. Kate worried she'd misstepped, but the intense focus in his eyes was the same as when he was begging to eat her pussy. He was turned on by this, she realized with surprise.

"You don't think I could take every dollar you've got?" she asked silkily. She pressed her hand to Mikhail's chest, pushing him back.

He retreated obediently, back and back and back until he bumped into the conference table. Kate closed the space between them, pressing the length of her body against his.

He gripped the edge of the table, bracing himself as he stared down at her, dark eyes flashing with heat. She curled his tie around her fist, keeping it taut.

"I'd take your card and I'd spend every last penny you have, and you would just have to watch me do it, because that's what you're for."

Mikhail swallowed hard. "Knyazhna," he said weakly.

She tugged on his tie, forcing him to bend down, bringing his face close to hers. "A good slave serves me with everything he's got."

Mikhail nodded earnestly, eyes glazing. "Yes, knyazhna, let me serve you."

"That's not how a slave talks to his princess." Kate released his tie, stepping back.

He sank immediately to his knees, clasping his hands behind his back and bowing his head. His suit stretched across the breadth of his shoulders and back, the brute strength there evident beneath layers of finely cut, expensive fabric. "Please, knyazhna, take my money. Take everything."

God, why was she getting turned on by this? Was she *that* materialistic? Probably. She shrugged the guilt away. Everyone had their flaws.

"Well, since you asked so nicely." She reached for the hem of her skirt, pulling it up in a slow tease. "How do you thank me?"

Mikhail looked up, eyes glazing further at the sight of her. Smiling, Kate hooked her finger in the gusset of her panties, already wet with her arousal, and pulled it to the side. Mikhail groaned and surged towards her, big hands clasping her thighs, face buried between them.

His enthusiasm almost knocked Kate backwards. She braced herself on the conference table with one hand and gripped his hair with the other. He moaned his pleasure as he tasted her, tongue stroking, circling, lips sucking.

Her orgasm came hard and fast, leaving her breathless and trembling. When it was over, she was slow to dismount, not certain her legs were solid enough to keep her upright. Mikhail's breaths gusted hot and heavy over her sensitive skin, face nuzzling gently against her mons.

Carefully, Kate disentangled herself from him, sliding her leg off his shoulder, but keeping her hands in his hair, stroking gently over his scalp instead of tugging. Her arousal glistened on his lips and chin and nose. The sight of him like this—normally hard expression now stunned, needy, openly vulnerable—filled Kate with soft affection. She reached over to where a box of tissues sat on the conference table and pulled one out. She moved to wipe his face clean, but Mikhail turned away from her tender ministrations.

"You don't have to do that."

She snatched his hair again, keeping him in place with careless cruelty. "If I want to keep my possession clean, then that's my prerogative, isn't it?"

He blinked, and the resistance was gone. He leaned against her again, quiet, docile, and compliant as she wiped his face clean. Dazed pleasure fogged his eyes. That feeling of affection surged again, and the impulse to kiss his softly parted lips was nearly impossible to resist. Instead, she stepped away from him, walking to the wastebasket and tossing the tissue in it.

"Stand up and take off your underwear," Kate said, turning back to him.

She watched as he complied, forced to unlace his shoes and step out of them in order to get his pants off, and then the dark, snug boxer briefs he wore underneath. His cock stood urgently to attention, thick and ruddy, as he bent to slide everything down his legs. He walked over to Kate, cock bobbing, and handed them to her, brow furrowed uncertainly.

Kate tossed them in the trash. "Now get dressed."

She waited while he got back into his pants, fastened his belt, stepped back into his shoes, and bent to lace them.

"Come here."

He stepped closer, stopping just in front of her. She grasped his hard cock through the fine weave of his trousers, giving it a possessive squeeze. Mikhail stiffened, hand shooting out to brace himself against the wall behind her.

"This is mine," Kate said with a mean smile. "You don't touch what's mine until I give you permission. Understand?"

He hauled in a shaky breath. "Yes, knyazhna."

"Good boy." She gave him one more squeeze, and then turned away, opening the door, and leaving him to his torment.

MIKHAIL REMAINED BRACED AGAINST THE WALL, breathing raggedly. His trousers rubbed against the hypersensitive head of his cock, driving him halfway mad. The need to stroke himself off was agonizing, but he resisted. It would be with him all day, a constant reminder of her power over him, every time he felt the slide of his trousers against his bare flesh.

This would be enough. He was confident. This insane, unprecedented need would be assuaged by more frequent contact. He'd be able to focus again, run his fucking company, instead of spending every waking minute anticipating the next time he could see her.

A more encompassing dynamic would help him burn through the lust faster, too. Or, at least, he hoped it would. These intermittent flare-ups of sexual need were generally an unwanted distraction, but with Kate Pasternak, it was a debilitating handicap. He couldn't think of anything but her. He couldn't get anything done. The sooner he exorcised his attraction to her, the better. He'd send her on her way with a generous severance gift, and they'd never have to cross paths again.

But for now, he was walking around with the exquisite agony of her denial, and it cleared his mind like nothing else. He went back to his office with renewed focus. He had a conference call in an hour to discuss the financials of a potential acquisition, and finally, he could do it with his head screwed on. Just yesterday, he'd sat through an entire board meeting without absorbing a single word that was said to him, responding on autopilot while his mind was consumed by desperate anticipation of when he could next kneel for Kate—when he could drop the world off his shoulders, empty his mind, and just obey.

And now, he had business in New York for a few days, but it no longer stretched ahead of him like a prison sentence. No matter where he went, Kate could command him.

Chapter Ten

As soon as Mikhail had given her broader authority over him, Kate wasted no time in testing it. There was nothing too absurd for her to demand of him. Friday night, she sent a text informing him that he had to wear red underwear the next day. Bright and early Saturday morning, he sent her a photograph of himself, standing in a hotel bathroom, wearing nothing but tight red boxer briefs.

Giddily pleased, she sent him another text.

> Good boy. Also, your socks are not allowed to match.

He responded with another picture—a black sock with a subtle stripe pattern on one foot, another black sock with a subtle diamond pattern on the other.

> Different colors.

Another picture—the black striped sock paired with a dark gray striped sock.

She grinned. He was being a brat on purpose.

> Brighter colors or I'll make you watch while I get myself off and you won't be allowed to touch yourself.

A very quick reply—a burgundy sock on one foot, a navy blue one on the other.

> There's a good boy.

SATURDAY MORNING, SHE RECEIVED THE BANK notification that her weekly five-thousand-dollar "gift" had been deposited. In a sunny mood, she texted Mikhail that he was allowed to dress as he pleased, but he had to get her permission before he ate or drank. Obediently, he texted her throughout the day, requesting permission for food and drink.

"Who's blowing up your phone?" Naomi asked after a string of texts in which Kate vetoed all of his drink requests—no to coffee, no to tea, no to coke, no to orange juice—until she'd finally permitted him water.

"Oh... uh. A guy." Shit. She should've said a "friend."

Naomi's brows rose with interest. "A *guy?* Like a romantic kind of guy?"

"No, more like a friends-with-benefits kind of guy." Boss-with-benefits, whatever.

ON SUNDAY MORNING, NAOMI HAD TO WORK, SO KATE was alone in the apartment. She commanded Mikhail to have lunch delivered to her from Violetta. She thought it'd be an impossible ask. Violetta was the most expensive and exclusive restaurant in the city. Reservations opened every three months, and they booked out in a matter of minutes every time. A place like Violetta did *not* do takeout. And they were only open for dinner hours. The idea of getting a takeout lunch from Violetta was laughable.

Kate hadn't demanded Violetta because she'd expected to get it. She'd demanded it because she wanted a reason to punish Mikhail. It'd been days since she'd left him hard and wanting in the conference room, and she wanted a reason to make him edge himself without being allowed to come while she watched over the phone.

But to Kate's astonishment, a courier buzzed her intercom at noon on the dot. Kate let him up and he appeared at her door with a heavy paper bag. Rich scents of garlic and butter and spices filled the air. Kate accepted the bag, peering inside at the nicest takeout containers she'd ever seen.

"This is... this is from Violetta?" she asked in quiet disbelief.

"Yes, ma'am," the courier answered. "Could you sign here, please?"

Still incredulous, she signed for the delivery.

Carrying the bag like it was filled with explosives, Kate went to her little kitchen table, nudged up against a window overlooking the street. She pulled out the containers and silverware—*real* silverware wrapped in a cloth napkin—and opened the containers as quietly as she could. There was a crisp side salad of simple greens dressed in the most delicious vinaigrette Kate had ever tasted, a thin green soup that smelled like old socks but tasted like heaven, a single scallop on a bed of some sort of colorful vegetable puree with a buttery sauce, a crispy little puck of what was essentially very fancy scalloped potatoes, roast duck breast medallions with a rich au jus, and a gorgeous pistachio and raspberry mille-feuille with flakes of gold leaf and rose petals decorating the top.

Kate ate slowly, without the distraction of her phone or a book, savoring every bite. She'd never had such perfect food. She hadn't known food this good existed. Memories of the shitty meals she'd had to sketch together as a kid kept rising, but Kate pushed them away, determined to enjoy this.

When she was done, she stared at the empty containers for a moment. Still somewhat in awe, she quietly slipped them back in the bag. She remained at the table for a while, toying with the handles on the bag, lost in thought. The food had been delicious—probably the best she'd ever had—but there was something else about it that was hitting her strangely.

It was the care.

It was maybe the first time in her life she'd been with someone who'd cared about fulfilling her needs. Her exes had all liked being dominated in bed, but in a selfish way, where Kate had to be both mistress and servant—in control of their pleasure, but expected to get her own satisfaction from the control alone.

She hadn't dated in a while because she'd started to wonder if she actually liked the things she thought she liked. If she *did* like dominating men, why did she find them so exhausting? Maybe all the neglect and chaos of her childhood had affected her more than she realized, and taking control with romantic partners was just a coping mechanism.

Well. Maybe it was. But Mikhail's style of submission

had proved one thing to her—she *did* like dominating men. But she needed a man who gave as much as he took. And Mikhail might only see her as a paid contractor, but he treated her the way she wanted to be treated. His submission prioritized *her* pleasure, and in return, she was desperate to return the feeling. The next time she saw him, she was going to make him come so much, he'd be begging her to stop.

With a small, wicked smile, she started cleaning up. She'd just put all the containers in the dishwasher—they were too nice to throw away—when the buzzer rang. She frowned, looking toward the intercom panel beside the front door. Anybody who might swing by usually called or texted first. Suspicious that she was going to have to turn away religious loons, she got up and tentatively pressed the speaker button. "Hello?"

"Hey, Trina. Let me in."

Kate's stomach dropped. Her blood turned to ice. "Angel?" she asked, desperate to be wrong.

"Who the fuck else would it be? Buzz me in, bitch."

"What are you doing here?"

"It's cold as balls out here," her sister snapped impatiently. "Let me in!"

Kate hesitated. Despite living only a couple of hours away in Milwaukee, Angel had never visited her in Chicago before. Kate hadn't seen her sister in person in more than three years. It felt absurd not to let her in, but her gut was telling her not to do it.

While she was deliberating, Angel laid on the buzzer. This close to the intercom, the sound was like a knife in Kate's eardrum. She flinched, clapping her hand over her ear.

She stabbed the button for the speaker, about to tell

Angel to fuck off, but Angel's voice drifted over, already speaking to somebody else.

"—my sister. Yeah. She lives here. Oh, thanks, I appreciate it."

The sound of the entry door swinging open and shut hit Kate like a slap. Some stupid motherfucker had let Angel into the building. She slumped against the front door, hand on the deadbolt, not sure what she was going to do. A few minutes later, she heard the sound of footsteps coming up the stairwell. She peered through the peephole, watching as Angel stepped into view.

Angel had changed a lot since Kate had last seen her. She'd lost a lot of weight—and she'd already been thin before. Her skin was dry and colorless, with small open sores scattered over her cheeks and forehead. She had a new tattoo on her left cheekbone—it was probably supposed to be a word or a name, but it was so badly done that it was just an illegible scribble. Her hair was dyed a deep, burgundy-plum color, but her blonde roots had grown out enough to make it look like she was balding. Her bright blue eyes looked unnatural and ghostly behind tangled, grown-out lash extensions. She raised her hand to knock on the door, revealing a set of brightly colored acrylics so badly in need of a fill that more of her nail bed was bare than painted.

Kate's lip curled. That haphazard, cheap-ass, no-taste, lazy attitude to her appearance permeated every other aspect of Angel's life. She acted without thinking. She made stupid choices and then tried to pretend the consequences didn't exist. She thought she was the baddest bitch around when, really, the rest of the world looked at her and saw a sad clown.

She was Kate's worst nightmare.

"TRINA!" she bellowed through the door, pounding on it with the side of her fist. "Open up, bitch! I know you're in there!"

Goddamn it. Kate couldn't make her neighbors listen to her sister's endless screaming. Gritting her teeth, Kate slid the deadbolt and ripped the door open.

"Well, hey, twinnie," Angel said with a smirk. She pushed her way into the apartment, using her weight to shoulder Kate aside despite the fact that she had to be at least twenty pounds lighter.

"What are you doing here?" Kate asked flatly, shutting the door. "I thought you were in jail."

"I got released. No thanks to you, you fucking cunt." She said it without any real heat, her attention focused on tracking over the details of Kate's apartment—the cleanliness, the matching furniture, the hardwood floors, the high ceilings, the framed art on the walls, the bookshelves.

It was the polar opposite of the single-wide trailers they'd grown up in, with their cracked faux-wood paneling and peeling-up linoleum and broken windows duct-taped over with cardboard and garbage bags. Angel let out a low whistle, walking deeper into the apartment.

"Take your shoes off!" Kate snapped. "Actually—no, don't. Because you're not staying."

"Oof, that's the thing." Angel flopped onto the couch. "I need a place to stay for a bit."

Kate nearly choked on her own lungs. "Absolutely fucking not."

Angel tilted her chin down, sending Kate a big-eyed, beseeching look. "Come on, twinnie. I need your help."

"Don't call me that." When they were kids, their dad had called them both "twinnie." It had taken Kate too long to realize that it wasn't a term of endearment—he just couldn't be bothered to remember which one of them was which.

"It's just a few days."

"No. Stay in your own place."

"Can't." She started shrugging out of her coat. "Got evicted."

"That's not my problem. Go stay with mom. Better yet— go visit Aunt Deb and see your fucking kids for once."

Angel's carefree expression dropped in an instant, replaced with the dead-eyed rage that had always terrified Kate when they were younger. When Angel got like that, there wasn't anything she wouldn't do. Kate still had a small scar on her chin where Angel had bashed her with a glass ashtray because Kate had gotten a bigger cookie.

Instinctively, Kate backed towards the bathroom door. She could lock herself in there if she needed. Angel's temper hadn't turned violent in years—not since high school—but Kate had very consciously limited contact since then, so that could've just been luck.

"Don't talk about my kids," Angel said in a harsh, low voice.

"Fine," Kate said, her voice brittle with anger and fear. "Then leave."

Angel got up from the couch, her fury still evident in the flatness of her expression. "You think you're so much better than me."

Yeah. She did. "Angel—"

Angel kept advancing. The bones of her face were too close to the skin, leaving her features sunken and sharp, making the deadness of her eyes all the more terrifying. Kate continued to back subtly towards the bathroom, trying not to tip Angel off that that's where she was headed.

"You came from the same shit hole I did!" Angel pointed her finger like a knife.

"I know." But Kate didn't stay there, rolling around in shit. She'd climbed out. "I still don't have anywhere for you to stay."

Angel stopped suddenly, the cold fury giving way to a much less terrifying flare of self-absorbed temper. "Jesus Christ, you have two fucking bedrooms!"

"I have a roommate! Am I supposed to kick her out for you?"

"I can sleep on the couch," Angel wheedled. She stomped back over to it, flopping down and crossing her arms with a stubborn expression. She wasn't going to move and there was nothing Kate could do to make her.

Or so Angel thought.

"Aren't you on parole right now?" Kate asked.

"So fucking what."

"I don't think you're supposed to cross state lines." Kate actually had no earthly idea what the law was, but she was a hundred percent certain that Angel didn't either, and it sounded plausible.

Angel's gaze sharpened on Kate. "Won't be a problem if I don't get caught."

"Well, if you don't want to get caught, you better get out of here."

"Why? You going to call the cops on me, *twinnie*?"

Kate hesitated. She wanted Angel gone. But she didn't want to be responsible for heaping more shit on her already shitty life. She could threaten to call the cops, and hope it was enough to scare Angel off. But if Angel called her bluff, then what?

Angel straightened, taking Kate's silence as an admission.

"Are you fucking serious right now? You would call the cops? For what? For sitting in your shit-ass apartment?" Her voice rose higher and higher with each word until she was screaming.

Kate gestured futilely for Angel to lower her voice. "My neighbors—"

"What do I fucking care?" Angel screeched, jumping to her feet. "Apparently I'm not going to be sticking around!"

"Angel, come on—"

"Fuck you! *FUCK YOU!*" Her scream was so shrill it warped in Kate's ear, a painful, broken wavering.

From the other side of Kate's living room wall, a heavy pounding sounded. "*Hey!*" her neighbor's voice, a grumpy older man named Mark Kowalczek, came muffled through the wall. "*Knock it off!*"

"Mind your own fucking business!" Angel screamed back at him.

Kate clutched her hands to her ears, wishing she could curl up in a little ball and hide in the closet like she used to do when she was a kid and Angel got out of control.

"Angel," she pleaded, "you have to go."

"I don't have to do fuck-all!" Angel slapped the lamp off the nearest end table. Ceramic and glass shattered as it hit the floor. She kicked the end table over, sending books flying. On the other side of the wall, Mark started pounding again. Kate's heart was beating like a hammer. Sticky, prickling sweat broke out over her whole body.

"*I'll call the cops!*" Mark shouted through the wall.

That got Angel's attention. "Fuck you, dickface!" She kicked the wall next to the couch, smashing a boot-shaped print through the plaster and lathe.

"Stop!" Kate cried.

Angel turned and stormed towards the door, slapping picture frames off the wall as she went. Glass shattered in her wake. "Tell that asshole not to bother," she snarled, kicking at the wall again, thankfully leaving only a dirty print. "I'm gone." She ripped the front door open and stormed out.

Kate stood frozen in place, staring through the open doorway, listening to the sound of Angel's footsteps retreating down the stairs and the thunderous drumbeat of her own heart.

A few seconds later, Mark appeared in the hallway. He peered into Kate's apartment. Bald-headed and mustachioed, he looked like Mr. Clean, if Mr. Clean was seventy years old and liked to wear knitted cardigans. He spotted Kate, and the agitated glare dropped off his face, bushy eyebrows rising.

"You okay?" he asked gruffly.

Kate nodded stiffly. "Yeah. I'm so sorry about that. I was trying to get her to leave."

Mark nodded. "Family?"

"Unfortunately."

"I've been there." He paused, scrunching his lips guiltily. "Er... sorry to say, I called the non-emergency line. They're sending police over."

Kate rubbed tiredly at her temple. "No, that's fine. It was the only thing that was going to get her to leave."

"I'll wait for them. Let them know it wasn't you."

The fact that the clarification needed to be made was crushing. To be fair, not many people would mistake Kate and Angel for each other these days, identical twins or not. Even so, Kate recognized Angel in herself, and seeing her again was torture. Kate was Dorian Gray, and Angel was her portrait in the attic. Or something like that.

"Thanks, Mark."

Chapter Eleven

Two cops showed up twenty minutes later, stone-faced and speaking to Kate with a degree of condescension that verged on belligerent. Apparently, Mark wasn't the only neighbor who'd called in a noise complaint. Kate tried not to react to their disdain, to rise above whatever they expected from the source of a noise disturbance call, but the urge to mouth off was simmering in her blood like itchy fire. She managed to keep her cool—if she lost it, she'd be no better than Angel. Impulsive, reckless, stupid.

They talked to Mark after her and, magically, after speaking to a *man* who supported her version of events, the condescension dropped. They stopped with the intimations about fines for noise violations and instead suggested she consider filing a restraining order against her sister.

Kate knew she wouldn't do that, but she told them she'd think about it, and finally, they left.

Alone again, she cleaned up the mess Angel had made, sweeping up broken glass and then going over the floor again with a damp rag to pick up any shards she might have missed. She dumped the shattered lamp in the trash and righted the end table. She wiped the dirty shoe print off the wall and then stared helplessly at the hole next to the couch.

Her stomach sank as she realized she'd have to explain it to Naomi. And she'd have to call building maintenance and explain it to them. Basically, she was going to have to broadcast her trashy origins to all and sundry.

Kate sank down onto the couch, pressing her forehead into the heels of her hands. Post-adrenaline nerves were making her whole body shake like she'd had too much caffeine. She wanted to scream, but she couldn't. She couldn't be like that.

Taking a deep breath, she reached for her phone and called Anna. Anna already knew all about Kate's family. She wouldn't be judgmental. She'd listen. She'd talk Kate out of the restless, disordered feeling that was making her mind race and her hands shake.

Except she wouldn't. The call went to voicemail. Swearing softly, Kate tossed the phone onto the coffee table.

She was staring blankly into space, willing her nerves to settle, when the phone lit up. She snatched it, expecting a message from Anna.

Instead, it was Mikhail.

I just landed in Chicago.

Ah. Here was an outlet for this cagey feeling.

Are you headed home right now?

I will if you command it.

Half an hour later, the call came in. Kate shut herself in her bedroom and climbed into bed, accepting the call. Mikhail filled the screen, naked and kneeling. The silver Marian medallion gleamed against his dark chest hair. He was half-hard, hands clasped behind his back, head bowed.

"Hello," Kate said softly. "Have you been a good boy for me?"

He looked up, eyes burning with excitement. "Yes, knyazhna."

"You haven't been touching *my* cock, have you?"

His eyes darkened, a shudder tracing down his back. His cock pulsed, growing harder, thicker. "No, knyazhna."

"That's my good boy," she purred, settling back against her pillows. "I reward good behavior."

Mikhail's breathing staggered, audible even through the phone.

"I'm going to let you come, but you have to follow my instructions."

"Yes, knyazhna."

She smiled. "Do you have any toys?"

"Yes. I have... several."

"Any that vibrate?"

"Yes. Two plugs, a cockring, several—"

"A vibrating cockring?" Kate sat up excitedly.

Mikhail grinned. "It can be controlled remotely."

Wicked heat unfurled in Kate's belly, sending shocks of anticipation up and down her spine. "You shouldn't have told me that. I wanted to reward you for good behavior, and now all I want to do is tease you until you're begging for relief."

Mikhail's grin dissolved into a look of dark longing. "Yes, knyazhna. Make me beg."

Kate considered the logistics. "I'll have to come over to get the remote."

"You are of course welcome, but you don't need a remote. It's controlled through an app."

She debated between the merits of being able to tease him in-person versus the fun of making him suffer from a distance. Finally, distance won out. She was wearing sweatpants and had no makeup on. She didn't feel like getting dressed and done up. "Send me the link for the app and then go get the cockring."

It was easy enough to follow the link Mikhail sent her, download the app onto her battered old tablet, then login with the password he gave her. When she looked back at her phone, Mikhail was kneeling again, a black silicone ring encircling the base of his shaft and balls.

"I'm going to test it." The controls had a slide to adjust the vibration intensity, and then a button that could be held down for however long she wanted the vibration to go. She set the slider on the low end and held the button down for a second.

Mikhail jerked, his cock twitching, and let out a harsh breath.

"It's working?" Kate asked, clenching her thighs together as delicious arousal built in her core.

"Yes, knyazhna," he said gruffly. "It's working."

"Alright. I'm going to ask you some questions. For each one you answer incorrectly, the length and the intensity of the vibration will increase. If you come before I say you can, I will make you lick your mess up. Understand?"

Mikhail's breathing roughened. "Yes, knyazhna."

"Good boy. First question—what's my middle name?"

"Rose."

Kate blinked. She hadn't expected him to know. "Er... yes. What's *your* middle name?" She asked mostly out of curiosity since she had no way of knowing if his answer was correct.

"I don't have one."

"You don't have a middle name?"

"Russians don't have middle names like Westerners do, with another given name. We have a first name, otchestvo, and surname."

"What's an otchestvo?" Kate asked, trying to pronounce the Russian word how he had.

"A name taken from the father's name. If your father's name is Ivan, your otchestvo will be Ivanovich or Ivanovna, depending on if you are a man or a woman."

"And what's your otchestvo?"

His gaze flattened. He didn't immediately answer. If this were a different question, she'd be giving him a buzz from the cockring. But she didn't feel right coercing personal information from him.

"Give me a color, Mikhail."

His gaze flickered as he looked away then back at her. "Green," he finally answered.

Relieved, she pressed the button down. Mikhail stiffened, bowing over and groaning. She held it for a count of three, then released it. "I asked you a question. What's your otchestvo?"

"I don't have one," he finally answered, his voice a low growl.

The otchestvo came from a person's father's name, and Mikhail didn't have one. Kate took that in for a second, not sure how to respond. The proud, wholesome proletariat father she'd imagined for him vanished in a puff of smoke.

Mikhail stared at her, expression shuttered, dark eyes like two cold stones.

"Alright," she said, forcing herself to slip back into the sultry domme persona. "Next question: what is my shoe size?"

Mikhail's brows lifted, expression thawing. After a moment's hesitation, he guessed, "Six?"

Kate laughed. "You don't know how women's shoe sizes work, do you? I'm five-foot-ten. I'd fall over if I had size six feet." She pushed the vibration intensity up a notch and laid on the button, watching with satisfaction as Mikhail grunted and doubled over again, breathing raggedly while she held the vibration for a count of five.

When she released him, he remained doubled over, panting.

"Proper posture," Kate said sharply.

He straightened immediately, eyes filled once more with dark heat, thick cock straining desperately upward.

"Next question: what's my favorite color?"

Mikhael's furrowed brow somehow furrowed even more. "Yellow?"

Kate raised the intensity and held the button for a count of ten. Mikhail groaned like a dying man, hands pressed to the floor, bracing himself up as he suffered through the teasing pleasure of the vibrations.

Kate released him. "Trick question," she said with a

wicked little laugh. "I don't have a favorite color." She tilted her head, surveying him through the phone screen, watching as he struggled to sit upright again. "Now, pay attention, because it's only going to get harder. What's my birthstone?"

Mikhail shook his head, his expression already pained in anticipation of failure. "Diamond?"

She sighed and raised the intensity, almost to the top of the slider now. "Points for the expensive guess, but no. It's topaz." She held down the button.

Mikhail's back arched, head thrown back as he moaned through the powerful vibrations. His cock pulsed as his hips rocked compulsively. Kate squeezed her thighs together, restlessly biting her lower lip as her pussy clenched.

"Knyazhna," he rasped. "I'm going to—"

"You better not. Not without permission."

"*Agh*, please, *pozhaluysta*, I can't—"

"You can." She'd lost count, but she figured that'd been at least twice as long as the last one. She released the button and Mikhail instantly slumped over. His broad back rose and fell with labored breaths.

"Fix that posture," Kate warned.

With a tortured sound, he managed to haul himself upright. His chest heaved as he struggled to breathe evenly.

"That's better. Now, there's one more question. If you make it to the end without coming, you'll get a reward. Ready?"

"Yes, knyazhna," he panted.

"This one's a yes or no question: do I make your cock hard?"

"Yes," he growled. "Yes, knyazhna. You make me so hard. Please, can I—"

"Oh no," Kate sighed, her face a mask of pity. "Oh dear, you got that one wrong."

Mikhail hesitated a second, his gaze distant as he traced over his words. "I... how?"

"The question was 'do I make *your* cock hard?' But that's not your cock, is it?"

Mikhail breathed out in haggard defeat, head hanging. "No, knyazhna."

"Whose is it?"

Another pained breath. "Yours."

"That's right." She slid the vibration intensity all the way to the top. "Remember not to come or you'll be in trouble." She held the button down.

Mikhail gave a startled shout as it hit him, bucking like he was going to get up. "*Ah!* Knyazhna!" He managed to stay on his knees, but his teeth were clenched in a snarling grimace, all the cords of his neck standing out in stark relief. His whole body trembled, hips rolling, muscles clenching. His cock pulsed again and again. His arms broke out of position behind his back, reaching instinctively for his cock.

"Ah-ah," Kate said cheerfully. "Hands behind your back."

He put them back, rolling his shoulders and groaning. "Please, knyazhna, I can't—I can't—*ah*, fuck. Fuck! Please, knyazhna, pozhaluysta—*agh!* Blyat. Fuck. I'm going to come!"

"You better not."

He let out an agonized moan, head falling back, his whole body trembling like a lathered stallion. He was beautiful. A big, powerful man made weak and needy, utterly at Kate's mercy. She cupped herself through her panties, feeling the slick wetness already seeping through. She watched as Mikhail writhed and moaned and begged, watched his tortured cock twitch and pulse and strain.

"Don't make me come, knyazhna," he pleaded. "Let me please you, please, please—"

Kate released the button. Mikhail sagged in relief. She immediately pressed it down again and he jolted as if he'd been struck by lightning, groaning out a stream of what could only be Russian profanity.

She wasn't sure if she wanted him to come or not. On the one hand, making him lick his own mess off the floor had its appeal. But on the other, she hadn't yet rewarded him for his good behavior over the last few days, and the urge was still strong.

After a few more seconds of torture, in which he managed not to break, she let off the button. When she didn't immediately press it again, Mikhail slumped over, gasping for breath, body trembling and gleaming with sweat. He remained on his knees, hands clasped behind his back. He was the perfect image of defeat. Vercingetorix at the feet of Caesar. Kate had always thought she'd make a good Emperor.

"Did you come?" she asked.

"No, knyazhna."

She smiled. "Good boy. Since you've been so good, I will let you choose your reward."

Before she could tell him his options, Mikhail raised his head to meet her gaze, expression earnest. "Come over, knyazhna. Let me please you. Let me feel you."

She was hot and bothered enough that the idea of getting dressed up and leaving the comfort of her apartment no longer bothered her. Even so, she wasn't going to hop to fulfill his request. She needed to make him work for it.

"You never gave me the credit card you promised. Why would I reward you with my body?"

"I'm sorry, knyazhna. I promise I'll have it for you soon. It takes a few days to process—"

Kate scoffed dramatically. "That sounds like an excuse."

"No, no, please, let me—let me take you shopping. I'll buy anything you want."

Kate hesitated, falling out of character for a moment. "People would see us together. You're famous."

Mikhail shrugged. "My name is famous. My face is not."

Kate gave him a skeptical look. Maybe he wasn't as immediately recognizable as a movie star, but he was still well-known.

"Trust me. The world only knows me in connection with my company. Out on my own, I am never recognized."

She thought about it for a moment, and finally, relented. "Alright. Fine. You can buy me things."

"Thank you, knyazhna. I'll pick you up in... forty minutes?"

Kate nodded. She was about to end the call when a wicked idea flashed into her mind. "Make sure you leave the cockring on."

Mikhail's gaze bored into hers through the phone screen, hot and dark and hungry. "Yes, knyazhna."

Chapter Twelve

"Stay in the car," Mikhail instructed the driver when he saw Kate step out of her building.

The driver, Nick Korsch, nodded a silent acknowledgment.

"And put the divider up."

As the soundproofed, opaque divider rose up between the front and rear seats, Mikhail stepped out of the vehicle and walked around to get Kate's door. When she spotted him, she froze mid-step, gaze widening as she looked up and down his body. After a stunned beat, she jarred herself back into motion, smiling ruefully as she neared him.

"You were right about not being recognized," she said.

Mikhail glanced down at himself. He was wearing jeans and a plain gray t-shirt beneath an old ski jacket. It was a far cry from how he dressed for the office. "I told you," he said, letting himself relax.

She reached up, flicking the brim of his Cubs hat. "You never struck me as a ball cap kind of guy, but..."

"But what?"

She smiled, playful and light. That smile did strange things to his chest. "But it really works for you."

He rubbed at his sternum, willing the giddy lightness away. "Why don't I seem like a 'ball cap kind of guy'?"

She shrugged. "You see a guy in a scruffy old Cubs hat, you don't expect him to have a Russian accent. Or own a multi-billion dollar company. Or drive a Bentley." She glanced at his driver. "I assume you don't want your staff to... overhear anything?" she asked quietly.

"As long as you don't shout, it will be fine. The divider is up."

She glanced at the car, her expression unreadable, then back at Mikhail. She didn't say anything, though, and simply slid into the open door. Mikhail closed it and went around to his side.

"Where would you like to go, knyazhna?"

She looked caught off guard by the question. "Um... I don't know. Michigan Ave?"

He pressed the intercom button built into his armrest so that he could speak to the driver. "Korsch, Michigan Avenue and Oak Street."

A moment later, the vehicle glided smoothly into traffic. Mikhail settled back against his seat, turning his attention to Kate. She was busy looking around the vehicle's interior with a guarded watchfulness that Mikhail recognized. The transition from immigrant grad student to CEO of one of the wealthiest companies in the world had been a strange and tumultuous ride. He'd adapted to the material comforts, maybe even come to take them for granted, but he still remembered the initial shock of finding out how differently the other side truly did live.

Well, he was on the other side now, and if it pleased

Kate, he would lavish what he could upon her until this choking obsession finally abated. Fuck, how he wanted it gone. And yet, the thought of it being over filled him with cold terror.

It would fade. It always faded. And when it did, the fear of losing her wouldn't even exist. Because he'd be done. He'd have gotten what he needed, and Kate would be just another happily compensated former companion. This particular arrangement had perhaps captured him a little more intensely than past arrangements, but that only meant that the satisfaction when it ended would be that much better.

Or so he told himself.

"You look distracted," Kate said.

He realized he'd been staring past her, out the window, in silence. When he returned his gaze to her face—a lovely face, cool and poised, with blue-hot fire in her eyes—he found that icy fear gripping him again. This would eventually end.

"Mikhail?"

He shook himself. "I'm sorry. I was lost in thought."

Kate considered him for a moment. A mild smile curled her lips. "I know how to help you focus." She pulled her phone out of her pocket. A second later, the cockring was buzzing around his shaft, sending little shocks of pleasure through his core. He drew in a fast breath, fingers curling on the armrest. His cock twitched, beginning to swell and stiffen. She had lowered the intensity back down to the mildest setting, but it wasn't the physical sensation that was making him hard. It was the knowledge that *she* was controlling it.

The vibrations stopped, though a ghost of the feeling continued to fizz through him.

"There we go. Now I've got your attention." She slipped the phone back into her pocket with a smirk.

"Oooh, I've been wanting a pair of noise-canceling headphones." Kate picked up a display model and examined them. They were baby blue with rose gold accents.

"Not those," Mikhail urged, reaching for a plain black model from a different brand. He handed the box to her. "These are better. Actually—" he pulled the box away before she could take it "—the selection here is not very good. Most of these are marketed for their aesthetic, not function."

Kate looked down at the pretty blue headphones in her hands. "I mean, I don't need the latest and most advanced in headphone technology." She wasn't a super discerning audiophile, and she cared more than a little bit about how nice the headphones would look while she was wearing them.

"Nobody *needs* it," Mikhail said impatiently. "But why would you settle for the lesser option when you can have the best?" He peered critically at the rest of the headphones. "This one isn't terrible," he said doubtfully, reaching for a different box. "But if you want the best—" He sucked in a sudden sharp breath, going still as a statue.

Kate stood next to him, phone out, thumb holding down the vibration button. "I want the blue ones."

Mikhail made a pained sound. "They're not—"

She dialed up the intensity of the vibration. "I don't think you heard me," she said with an innocent smile. "I like the blue ones."

"Knyazhna—"

She increased the intensity again. He gripped the display shelf, breathing shallowly.

"Are you going to give me what I want, or do I have to—"

"Can I help you guys?"

Kate's eyes went wide as saucers. She immediately let off the vibration, shoving her phone into her pocket as she turned to face the approaching salesman. Mikhail said nothing, still leaning heavily on the shelf as he regained his breath.

Kate pasted on a polite smile. "Oh, no thanks, we're just—"

"We'll take the blue headphones," Mikhail said unsteadily.

Kate couldn't help the saturnine smile that took over her face.

Several hours later, in addition to the headphones, Kate had gained an iPad, a gorgeous Valentino handbag, several sets of very expensive lingerie from an appointment-only boutique (which Mikhail was able to secure in seconds with a brief call to his assistant), a Patek Phillipe watch with a rose gold bezel and diamonds surrounding the face, and a beautiful perfume whose price had nearly choked Kate when she saw the receipt. Mikhail paid for it all unflinchingly, ignoring when Kate balked at the expense, and carried all the bags like a hired porter.

When they were alone, out of sight and sound from others, Mikhail provoked her by insisting on different colors or styles or brands from the things she wanted, and she tortured him into compliance with the cockring. It wasn't something she risked in smaller boutiques, but in Neiman Marcus and Saks, she found herself battling wills with him every time they found themselves in an empty aisle or discreet corner.

"I didn't realize you were such a brat," Kate said conversationally, holding down the vibration button. Mikhail leaned against the wall, breathing roughly, eyes screwed shut, hands filled with Kate's shopping bags. "Here I thought you wanted to please me."

He gasped as she released the vibration. Hauling in a ragged breath, he let it out on a huff of laughter. "I *know* I'm pleasing you, knyazhna."

She smiled impishly, uninterested in pretending otherwise, and looped her arm through his, towing him back to the front of the store. "Well, I do enjoy your agony."

Mikhail made a gruff sound, deep in his throat—a pleased hum that also somehow sounded like a growl.

As they stepped out onto the sidewalk, Kate ambled aimlessly, interest in shopping waning. They'd been at it for hours, and while she was thrilled to have beautiful things that she would've never expected to own, there was an edge of discomfort that came with it too. Kate was ostensibly in charge, Mikhail serving her with his wallet, but the power of that wallet was immense. With every outrageous purchase, Kate became more and more aware of how wildly disparate their lives were. And while she felt no shame taking money from him—he'd hardly notice the loss—she couldn't help feeling a small ding to her pride that she was only able to get these things because a man had deigned to bestow them upon her.

And even worse—this was just a sexual thing for him, but Kate was getting overwhelmed again by the same soft, glowing feeling that the lunch from Violetta had imparted. It didn't help that he looked so different today. So ordinary. Like he was actually the type of guy Kate might reasonably expect to date. She preferred the suits, not because she necessarily thought they looked better, but because they imposed a certain remove between the two of them. In a suit, he was the CEO of Domovoy. Wealthy. Mysterious. Unknowable. In jeans and a beat-up old baseball cap, he looked... real. Touchable. Familiar.

"What are you thinking, knyazhna?"

"Hm?" Kate looked up, pulled out of her thoughts. Mikhail was watching her with an unnerving acuity. She wasn't about to admit to her sentimental confusion. "Oh—uh, nothing."

He raised his brows skeptically.

"Seriously, nothing." She looked away from him, focusing her attention on the stores they were passing. The nearest was an upscale cookware store, a display of colorful Le Creuset in the window. "Oh, look," she said, desperate to change the conversation. "I've always wanted one of those Le Creuset pots."

That was true, actually. Despite the fact that she couldn't really cook anything more complex than Hamburger Helper, she'd always wanted nice kitchen things—and to know how to use them. People who had Le Creuset pots and fancy stand mixers and good knives were the sort of people who were on speaking terms with their fathers and had bachelor's degrees and good credit scores and just generally had their shit together. Kate wanted to be one of those people.

Without a word, Mikhail steered Kate into the store.

"Oh—no, wait. I don't need—" She wasn't sure why she was objecting now. An enameled cook pot would be the cheapest thing she'd gotten today.

"Hello! How are you?" They were greeted by a young woman wearing a black apron over her button-down shirt and charcoal trousers.

"Good, thank you," Kate said automatically.

"Is there anything I can help you find?"

"Oh, no, we're just—"

"She wants the Le Creuset pot," Mikhail cut in.

The saleswoman nodded in immediate recognition. "The dutch oven?"

"Um..." Why couldn't she say yes? Why was the pot freaking her out more than the ten-thousand-dollar watch?

"Yes," Mikhail answered firmly.

"All of our Le Creuset is over here." She led them to a wall filled with colorful enameled cookware. "This is the dutch oven. These two," she laid a hand on two different display models, one slightly larger than the other, "are our most popular sellers."

Kate stared blankly at them.

Mikhail nudged her. "Which one do you want, knya—" he cut himself off, gaze flicking briefly to the saleswoman. "Katya?" he said instead.

Katya. That warm glow that had been simmering in her chest suddenly expanded. It was choking her to keep it contained. She wasn't sure what would happen if she let it spill over, but she was terrified to find out.

"That one," she said, pointing blindly at one of the two displays.

"Awesome," the saleswoman said brightly. "Color?"

"This one?" she gestured to a deep indigo-blue, the first color that caught her eye on the display.

"I *love* that color," the saleswoman gushed, bending to pull a box off the shelf. "If you guys are ready, I can take you to the register, otherwise I can keep this until you're done."

"Um..." Kate was suffocating on that warm feeling. In normal people, it was probably a good feeling, but Kate was starting to feel hot and itchy and like she wanted to sprint out of the store.

"We'll keep looking," Mikhail said.

Kate allowed herself to be guided past the Le Creuset, towards a locked display of Wüsthof knives.

"Are you alright?" Mikhail asked softly.

Ah, fuck, why did he have to do that? He wasn't allowed to be sweet and perceptive. She couldn't handle it on top of everything else. "I'm fine," she said briskly.

She forced herself to slip back into the spoiled princess persona, and by the time they left the store, Kate was the slightly unsettled new owner of a Le Creuset dutch oven, a hand-forged steel Santoku knife, a set of Waterford crystal water goblets, and—just because Mikhail was getting mouthy —a set of mother of pearl caviar spoons (despite the fact that she'd never eaten caviar in her life).

"You should try caviar the Russian way," Mikhail said, examining the fancy little spoons with amused skepticism.

"Is that when I make a certain Russian feed it to me?"

Mikhail chuckled. "I wouldn't object."

Kate could think of at least eighty million things sexier than being spoon-fed fish eggs, and she couldn't help the grimace that crossed her face.

He laughed again.

As they spilled back out onto the sidewalk, Mikhail loaded down with an absurd amount of bags and boxes, Kate's arm looped habitually through his, that unpleasant glowy feeling started to overwhelm her again. She stared at all the things he'd gotten her and a hard lump rose in her throat. She didn't know why, but her eyes started to sting. She turned away from Mikhail, pretending to stare at passing store windows, while hot tears trickled down her cheeks.

"Knyazhna?"

"Hm?" She kept her gaze fixed on a passing window display of men's suits.

"What's wrong? Look at me."

She was glad his arms were loaded down with a dutch oven and a multitude of bags. It meant he couldn't reach for her, couldn't make her look at him.

Or so she thought. With his long-legged stride, he easily cut in front of her, bringing her up short. Her head jerked up in surprise, her wide-eyed gaze meeting Mikhail's for a stunned second before she twisted away from him. Despite all his cargo, Mikhail managed to snake a hand out and catch her by the arm. He reeled her in towards him, his face set in grim lines as he searched hers.

"What's this?" he asked, brows drawn together. "You're crying?"

"It's nothing. Honestly. Just ignore me."

A hint of distress broke through his stoic expression. "No crying, Katya."

Oh, for fuck's sake. The new nickname just brought the tears on harder.

Mikhail made an alarmed sound, swearing under his breath in Russian.

"Sorry," Kate said thickly, wiping at her cheeks, breathing deeply to get herself back under control.

"Is there something else you want?" Mikhail asked urgently. "Tell me what it is, we'll get it."

Oh, god. The tears resurged with a vengeance. She pressed her hands over her face, mortified. "No," she said, her voice watery and hoarse. "I'm honestly fine."

"Please stop crying," he pleaded with the panicked air of

a man who was suddenly in way over his head. "Are you hungry? Will food help?"

He wanted to buy even more for her? More gifts? She swallowed a snuffling sob.

The part of her that had always remained detached, watchful, vigilant—even as a child—was alert now. *They're not gifts*, that part of her mind whispered. *They're payment. And you aren't holding up your end of this transaction. He's not paying you to have feelings—especially not feelings that make him uncomfortable.*

Taking one deep breath after another, Kate fought for control. She needed to fix this. She needed to get a grip or she was going to ruin this arrangement. If she couldn't be the powerful, in-control princess when she was with Mikhail, then he could easily find somebody else who could. If he put out an open call, the line of women wanting to take Kate's place would be miles long. She couldn't indulge her weaknesses around him. She had to save her neurotic break-downs for at home, in private.

She suppressed the chaotic emotional jumble until it was just an erratic drum beat at the back of her mind, wiped away her tears, and let out a small huff of laughter. "No, I'm not hungry. I'm just PMSing. Sorry."

"You're... alright now?" Mikhail was watching her like she was an unexploded ordinance he'd just found on the sidewalk.

"Yeah, I'm fine," she said flippantly. "Don't look so scared. If you're going to serve a princess, you're going to have to deal with a few mood swings."

Some of the tension eased from Mikhail's posture. "Do you need anything for your, er... PMS?"

"Yes. Ice cream." What she really wanted was to go home, but she had to play this out.

The rest of Mikhail's tension fled as his eyes lit up. "Ah. That I can do."

BACK AT HER APARTMENT, LOADED DOWN WITH shopping bags and the heavy dutch oven—because allowing Mikhail into her apartment felt too intimate—Kate found a folded paper tucked into the edge of the door. Fumbling to hold everything, she opened the door, and the paper fluttered to the ground. She carried her new things to the kitchen island and dumped them there before coming back for the paper. The bubbly handwriting was instantly recognizable as her sister's.

> *Hey twinnie,*
> *Sorry. I've been trying to get better at not losing my*
> *shit like that. I don't have any money right now, but I*
> *think I will in a few weeks. I know you blocked my*
> *number, but Mom said you still talk to her, so tell her*
> *how much all your stuff costs that I broke so I know*
> *how much I owe you.*
> *—Angel*

Kate looked past the paper to the heap of expensive gifts on the kitchen island. Her gaze landed on the dutch oven, and a knot tightened in her throat.

Angel had always been the one to figure out food. When they were kids, on the nights when they'd been left alone with a mostly empty fridge and no money to buy anything, Angel somehow managed to scrape meals together for them both. Angel was the one who'd figured out how to use the stove at six years old, without any instruction, when Kate had been too scared to try. Angel was the one who'd come up with the idea to hide stuff in the freezer behind the bags of ice so that they had backup food stored away for those days when Dad went too long without getting groceries. Angel was the one who learned, through trial and error, how to make plain things like condensed soup and frozen peas and canned tuna into meals that actually tasted good. And she'd done it with dinged-up old aluminum pots, chipped mixing bowls, and broken utensils.

Kate hardly knew how to cook, and now she had a fucking Le Creuset dutch oven while Angel apparently had nowhere to live.

She dropped her face into her hands, angry at herself, angry at the world, and crying—*again*. She wasn't normally this emotional. In fact, she'd always considered herself some-what detached. Maybe even a little too detached. But not lately. She dragged in a stuttering breath, eyes squeezed shut against a flood of hot, stinging tears.

She stiffened at the sound of a key turning in the front door.

Naomi came in with a heavy sigh, swinging the door shut and muttering to herself. "...might as well join a convent if this is what—oh! Kate? Oooh, what's all this? Did you go shopping?"

Kate was struggling to rearrange her features into a neutral expression, even though it was futile. Her whole face was hot and tight from crying, her eyes still stinging.

"Yep," she said, moving to gather some of the bags so she could take them to her room and maybe somehow keep her face averted the whole time.

"Oh, wow, is that a Saks bag?" Naomi moved closer. "Was there a big sale or something?"

"Um, yeah." Kate tried to move past Naomi, but Naomi stopped her with a hand on her elbow.

"Hey, are you—oh no. Kate, what happened? What's wrong?"

"Nothing. Just being emotional."

Naomi frowned, lips pursing uncertainly. "Is there something I can do?"

"Honestly? Just pretend everything's normal." Kate swiped hastily at her wet cheeks.

"Are you sure?"

Kate nodded, drawing in a slow breath.

"Alright. Well..." Naomi glanced around the apartment, at a loss. "Uh... want to watch another episode of Stupid Cupid? The new one's out."

Absurdly, the thought of that dumb show lifted Kate's mood. "Yeah. That sounds good. Give me one second while I put this stuff away."

She went into her bedroom and dumped all the bags on the bed. Pulling out her phone, she sent a quick message to her mom: *Tell Angel she doesn't owe me anything.*

Chapter Thirteen

His fixation on Kate Pasternak was becoming a problem.

The sight of her crying had been burned into his brain, and it kept cropping up at inopportune moments. Every time, he was overcome with the urge to call her, to see her, just to make sure she wasn't crying.

And if she was... then what? Panic again? Buy her more ice cream? He wasn't emotionally equipped to comfort another person, but Kate's tears had gotten under his skin like acid and now he couldn't stop wondering *why* she'd been crying. Maybe it had been hormones, like she claimed, but still, *something* had to have been the catalyst. Was it something he'd done?

"*—sent him the numbers, and he agreed with Roberts. It's not worth the risk. So, obviously, the decision is yours, but the reports are all pretty conclusive.*"

Mikhail pulled his phone away from his ear for a second, suddenly aware that he'd sat through an entire conversation without absorbing a single word, distracted by thoughts of the sorceress he'd mistakenly sold his soul to. He suppressed a growl of frustration and brought the phone back to his ear.

"We'll discuss it more when I get back from Shanghai. I have to let you go, we're about to land."

They were about to do no such thing. His jet was still somewhere over Siberia. The far eastern reaches of his fatherland. His hand went to his throat, loosening his tie so that he could reach into his collar and pull out the silver chain he always wore. He gripped the Marian medallion, stroking his thumb pensively over the engraved surface. The warmth of the metal, the familiar feel, soothed his agitated mind. He stared out the window, seeing nothing but cloud cover below, and night sky above.

His phone buzzed and he reached for it, dropping the medal as soon as he recognized the name on the screen—Княжна. *Knyazhna.*

Have you been good today?

Mikhail glanced at his watch, still set to Chicago time. It was seven in the morning there. The corner of his lip crooked up into an unintentional smile. Was this the equivalent of a "good morning" text?

Of course I have. I'm always good.

Her reply was immediate.

I think you know that I need proof.

Suppressing a smile, he got up and went to the lavatory at the back of the jet. Inside, he flipped his tie over his shoulder and unbuttoned his shirt. He pulled it open and tugged up his undershirt, revealing the smudged message written across his abdomen in permanent marker: *Property of Kate*. She'd written it on him after more than an hour of increasingly torturous edging in which she'd sat primly in his office chair while he knelt before her, and commanded him to stroke himself—stopping him every time he got close to coming. When she'd finally let him come, the shattering pleasure had nearly killed him. He'd been slumped against the wall, trying to remember how to breathe while Kate uncapped a marker and labeled him as hers.

"Don't wash this off," she'd commanded silkily. "Or there'll be consequences."

And then, like two civilized human beings who hadn't just made each other sweaty and sticky, they'd sat down for a few rounds of chess. Mikhail had won all three. The exact traits that made Kate so natural at taking control were her fatal flaws when it came to chess. Too aggressive, too impatient, too bold.

She was perfect.

The sight of her mark on his skin, the reminder of her ownership, sent a hot bolt of arousal straight to his groin. At the same time, something softer, heavier, thicker, pushed against the inside of his sternum. He pressed a hand there, frowning. He had perfect blood pressure and good cholesterol levels. And besides, heart attacks were supposed to hurt.

His phone screen lit up with another message from Kate.

If I don't see proof in the next five minutes,
I'll have no choice but to punish you.

That heavy feeling lingered in his chest, but he ignored

it, opening the camera on his phone to send Kate a picture of her handiwork.

Good boy.

He could hear the smirk in her voice, even in text.

Three days in Shanghai, then two in Tokyo, then back to Chicago. Just five. Five days until he could see her again. It was too long. Could he convince her to quit her job and take a full-time salary to travel with him? He'd have to give her some kind of job title that she could use on a resume. Their arrangement would eventually end, as all things did, and she'd need to find other work. Something related to her field.

He already had a personal assistant, who also had her own assistant. His homes were overseen by a household manager who supervised the personal chef, groundskeepers, and housekeeping staff. On the business side of things, he had two executive assistants who were supported by their own army of staff as well. What position could he possibly invent that wasn't already covered by all those roles?

"Sarah?" Mikhail said as he returned to his seat.

His personal assistant, Sarah Engels, was seated on the other side of the aisle, with her laptop open on the lacquered table in front of her. She was only in her late twenties, but she was brutally efficient, entirely unsentimental, and could be trusted to help cover up mass murder—not that he'd put the last one to the test.

She looked up at the sound of her name. "Yes?"

"What kind of support staff could be added to my current team?"

She frowned. "Are you unhappy with somebody's performance?"

"No. I want to add a role. In addition to what I already have."

Her frown deepened. A moment later, it resolved. "Ah." She nodded knowingly, not a trace of judgment in her expression. "Something for Kate Pasternak?"

"Yes." Mikhail didn't discuss his personal life with her, but Sarah had managed enough of the details of his last two arrangements—payments, reservations, gifts—in addition to the current one with Kate, that she certainly understood the nature of the relationships.

"Do you need an answer right away?" Sarah asked.

He shook his head. "No."

"Then I'll do some research, figure out what looks plausible." She paused. "And legally above board."

"Thank you." He returned his attention to his phone, bringing up Kate's texts again.

I'm always good for you, Knyazhna.

Chapter Fourteen

"What are you grinning about over there?" Anna asked, shooting Kate an amused, but suspicious look.

Kate hastily tucked her phone into her back pocket. While Mikhail had a few free hours in Shanghai, she'd been sending him on a silly scavenger hunt—giving him commands like, *find something green and round*, and, *find something small and hot.*

For the first, he'd sent her a picture of an arched bridge over green water. The arch was reflected in the still water, which in turn reflected light against the underside of the bridge, creating the illusion of a perfect green circle. For the second, he'd sent a picture of cubes of meat being grilled on skewers at a street vendor's cart. It was a fascinating way to see a part of the world she'd probably never be able to visit.

For her most recent command, *Find something tall and thorny*, he'd sent a picture of himself. He was stone-faced, as always, but there was a glimmer of humor in those dark eyes.

You're not thorny.

I thought it said horny.

It was such a stupid joke and Kate should have seen it coming from a mile away, but the fact that it had come from *Mikhail* had caught her completely by surprise, and she'd nearly laughed out loud right there at Anna and Jason's table. She was lucky she'd managed to restrain herself to a manic grin. She'd been halfway through a reply when Anna had caught her.

"Nothing," she said lamely.

"It's a man," Theo said with bored certainty.

Anna brightened, leaning forward. "Really? Who? What's he look like?"

"It's not a man," Kate lied with such obvious transparency, she might as well have said, "It's definitely a man."

Everyone laughed at her, even Jason. She gave him a wounded look. *Et tu, Brute?* But he just shook his head, grinning through that thick black beard.

"Alright, fine, it's a man. But it's not serious."

"Is this the friends-with-benefits guy who was blowing up your phone last week?" Naomi asked from the other side of the table.

Kate glared at her. "Wow. That was a complete violation of our roommate agreement."

Naomi's eyes went wide. "What? I'm sorry, I didn't—"

"You broke the seal of confession." Kate shook her head sternly.

"She's not a priest," Theo put in, amused.

"What happens now?" Anna looked cheerfully between Kate and Naomi. "Is she defrocked?"

"How do you defrock a roommate?" Jason asked. "Wouldn't that be eviction?"

"She can't defrock me," Naomi objected. "I'm on the lease."

Kate silently patted herself on the back for her artful diversion while everyone else debated a suitable analogue. When the conversation began to peter out, Kate gestured impatiently at the game board in the middle of the table. "Are we going to finish playing, or what?"

"It was *your* turn," Theo pointed out.

"Oh. Right." She quickly scooped up the dice before the conversation could return to what, exactly, had distracted her from the game in the first place.

Through sheer force of will, Kate managed to ignore her phone for the rest of the night. That didn't mean thoughts of Mikhail weren't running on an endless loop in her mind.

After her minor breakdown, Kate had managed to bundle up all those murky feelings and shove them into a deep, dark, easily-forgotten corner of her brain. She'd had a brief relapse into inexplicable moroseness when the promised credit card was delivered by courier, but she'd managed to shove that into the dark corner with all the other emotional instability.

As if to prove to herself that she was unbothered, Kate had taken the card on an online shopping spree. It had been unexpectedly heavy in her hand, matte black with a brushed metal finish. With it, she was now the half-hearted owner of some outrageously expensive clothes. They were an exorbitant expense to Kate, but she couldn't help looking at them through the lens of Mikhail's vast wealth, which made their cost seem downright paltry.

She'd briefly floated the idea of buying a Maserati, or a

house, something that might actually make him take notice, but then nixed it. First of all, despite the fact that her unlimited credit limit was backed by a literal billionaire, she wasn't sure you *could* buy a car with a credit card. Or a house. And secondly, even if she could, how would she explain those things to her friends?

"Kate."

She looked up, suddenly aware that she'd gotten lost in her own thoughts again. Everyone was looking at her expectantly. It must be her turn again. She reached for the dice as if she'd been paying attention all along, and rolled them.

Somehow, she managed to keep her head in the game after that. It was another cooperative game. This one something to do with terraforming inhospitable planets. Theo seemed to be subtly sabotaging the rest of the team out of pure boredom, so Kate focused on thwarting Theo's treachery. When Theo realized that Kate had caught on to his machinations, he doubled down, making more and more damaging moves with every turn. They ended up in their own game within the game, while the others played around them, oblivious.

At the end of the night, Theo was the first to leave. He grabbed his coat and punched Kate on the shoulder as he passed her. At the kitchen door, he ruffled up Anna's hair. He darted out while she was gasping in outrage, shouting his goodbye from the dark.

"He thinks he's *so* funny," Anna grumbled as she finger-combed her hair back into place. Her gaze landed on Kate and Naomi, slipping their coats on. "Oh! Hey. Before you guys leave—" She reached for a manila envelope on the kitchen counter and reached inside to pull out some papers. "The Margaret's Arms women's shelter is facing a major funding shortage. Their biggest donor pulled out when he found out they refer women for abortion services. If they don't make up the shortfall, they'll have to shut down, and more than eighty women and children will be homeless. If you can spare a little bit of cash, we can at least get them through the next month or two while they try to build up their donor pool."

Kate took the papers Anna handed her—a list of names, along with pledged amounts of money. Mostly women's names, mostly donations of less than fifty dollars.

"How much do they need?" she asked, continuing to stare at the names.

"For the year? About sixty thousand." Anna grimaced at the number.

Kate quickly tallied up the accumulated donations so far —not even three thousand dollars. The Maserati she'd been considering buying, to provoke Mikhail, had an MSRP of over a hundred and fifty thousand.

"What's this place called again?"

"Margaret's Arms," Anna answered. "They do really good work. A friend of mine is on their board of directors. She's a public defender and she's one of the smartest, most compassionate people I know. If she thinks—"

"I thought *I* was the smartest, most compassionate person you knew," Kate interjected lightly, still not able to tear her eyes away from the list of donations.

Anna snorted. "Smartest maybe."

"Theo's not the smartest?" Naomi asked sincerely.

Kate finally managed to tear her attention off of the paper, shooting Naomi an offended look.

"Sorry," Naomi said with a sheepish smile. "I grew up with Anna and Theo—he was valedictorian and everything."

Kate scoffed. "Big whoop." She handed the donation sheet back to Anna. "I'll get back to you about a donation. I have to check on something first, okay?" She had to figure out if she could fund a non-profit from a credit card.

AT HOME, KATE FINALLY HAD THE PRIVACY TO RESPOND to Mikhail. After she'd left his last message on read, he'd sent her a new picture of bright orange roses climbing an arching trellis. A little later, another message followed.

> I have a meeting now. I'll be unreachable for a few hours.

> How did your meeting go?

A split second after she hit send, her lungs shriveled with mortification. She shouldn't have sent him such a casual, girlfriend-y type text. She clutched her phone, trying to think of something else to add, to shift the tone back.

Before she could come up with something, Mikhail's reply came in.

> It was fine. Signed an agreement for manufacturing rights to a new processor that we're releasing next year.

She hadn't expected him to respond so casually.

> Is that a big deal?

> Not really. Business as usual.

A second later, he added:

When news gets out, company stock will shoot up. Good news for shareholders.

Kate's eyebrows rose. This conversation was so... ordinary. Well, except for the fact that she was having it with Mikhail Volkov. But otherwise, chatting casually with him about his workday? Not something they'd engaged in before. It felt very much outside the bounds of the princess-servant dynamic.

I'd buy stock, but I think that'd be insider trading.

I wouldn't tell.

She couldn't help but smile, though it faded a little at his next message.

I'll give you stock. A gift.

That sounds illegal.

It's not.

She had no idea how much Domovoy stock was worth right now. But if she sold any shares he gifted her, maybe she could give money to the shelter Anna was trying to save. It sounded excessively convoluted when she had a much simpler option.

I don't want stock. I want you to donate 60k to a nonprofit I care about.

Mikhail didn't respond right away. After a few minutes, his message finally came in.

> That's a lot of money.

Time to bring the domme out.

> I wasn't asking you, I was telling you. I'd do it with the credit card, but it's easier for me if you just donate the funds directly.

> 60k???

She smiled. She'd made the impression she'd wanted to.

> That's nothing to you. You're worth over fifty billion.

> The vast majority of my net worth is tied to the value of my shares of Domovoy. It's not cash in hand.

> What happened to the rich man who couldn't be bankrupted by little old me? I'll take the credit card and buy the Maserati I've had my eye on. You'll be wishing you hadn't mouthed back about the donation.

> I would rather you bought the Maserati.

Kate hesitated, confused.

> The Maserati costs over 100k.

> Get it.

Realization dawned on her. He didn't care about dropping sixty thousand dollars. He cared that he wasn't dropping it on Kate.

I hate to be the bearer of bad news, but you are in for a serious punishment when you get back.

Why?

Talking back. Ignoring commands.

What command?

I want that 60k donation. You don't get to come until it's made.

A long pause. Finally:

Where is the donation going?

Margaret's Arms Women's Shelter in Chicago.

Give me a minute.

Kate's heart seemed to swell. She held her breath, waiting for her phone screen to light up again.

He finally replied:

It's taken care of.

A wide, crazy smile stretched across her face. She whooped with excitement, spiking her phone against her bed like a football.

"Are you okay?" Naomi called from her own bedroom.

"Fine," Kate called back, embarrassed. To Mikhail, she sent:

That's much better. Doesn't it feel good to do as you're told?

Yes, knyazhna.

You're still in for a punishment.

That's only fair. I have time now.

Are you alone?

Yes.

Kate video called him. Mikhail answered immediately.

"Hello, knyazhna." He was wearing a suit, though he'd loosened the tie. Behind him, a large window looked out over a towering city center. Morning light glinted off of glass and metal skyscrapers, visible through a faint haze.

"Where are you?" she asked, eyeing the sleekly furnished room visible on the periphery of the screen.

"My hotel room," Mikhail answered.

"Take your clothes off," she said, keeping her voice low so that Naomi wouldn't hear her.

He propped the phone on whatever surface he'd been seated at—a desk or table of some sort—and stepped back, keeping his big body in frame as he undressed. When he was stripped bare, he stood for Kate's perusal, his cock slowly rising to attention.

"Stroke yourself," Kate ordered.

He let out a mild groan, already aware of where this was going, but did as he was told. He took himself in hand and slid his grip up and down his shaft.

"Faster."

He huffed out a breath, but obeyed.

"Don't come," Kate warned him.

"Knyazhna—"

"Shhh. Keep stroking. Tighten your grip."

Kate talked him through bringing himself to the edge, again and again. She slipped her hand between her thighs to cup herself, using the heel of her hand to grind against her clit. She lifted her phone to let Mikhail see what she was doing to herself. A feral noise tore from his throat, his hand working faster and harder over his cock.

"Don't come," Kate warned him, a little breathless with her own rising arousal. She was close, but she didn't let herself tip over the edge just yet. Instead, she continued to direct Mikhail. When he was shaking and slurring out Russian curses, pre-come slicking his hand and shaft, she couldn't take it anymore. Her orgasm crashed over her, making her back arch and her legs shake. She bit her lip, holding her breath so that she didn't cry out.

"*Knyazhna*," Mikhail snarled, hand braced on the table in front of the phone as he continued to stroke himself.

"Stop," Kate whispered.

He groaned and folded over, one hand braced on the table as he drew in shuddering breaths.

"We're going to repeat this every day until you return to Chicago," she told him brightly.

"Knyazhna..." His voice broke on a jagged whimper.

"That'll teach you to argue with me about how I want money spent, won't it?"

"Yes," he breathed harshly. He took a long moment to collect himself, gripping the edge of the table like he might fall over otherwise. When his breathing had evened, he pulled the chair out and slumped into it, his dark gaze meeting Kate's through the phone screen. His bare chest rose and fell like a slow bellows, the Marian medal glinting against that dark pelt of chest hair.

"I wish I'd brought you with me," Mikhail mused.

Kate's heart made a little sideways lurch. "You couldn't," she said. "I have to work."

Mikhail considered her for a moment. "I could make it so you didn't have to."

"People would be suspicious if the CEO was granting extra vacation days to some random logistics coordinator."

"I'm not talking about vacation. You wouldn't have to work at all."

Kate stared at him. "You want me to be your kept woman?" Two conflicting feelings raged inside her. The abject fear of ever letting herself be dependent on somebody else's care battled fiercely with the longing to be taken care of, to live in luxury without a single concern for money.

"No, no," Mikhail said softly, and her heart sank. A second later, it rose again as he said, "*You* would keep *me*, knyazhna."

———

Kate was at the bank of mailboxes in the lobby of her apartment building when her phone lit up with a call from Anna.

"Hello?" she answered, tucking her mail into her bag and locking her mailbox back up.

"Oh my god," Anna breathed. "Remember last night I asked if you could donate anything to the women's shelter that was going to be closed down?"

Kate went stone still. "Um... oh yeah. Sorry, I must've forgotten about it. I can come by with some money—"

"No need!" Anna crowed. "I just talked to Jasmine—she's on the board—they just landed the biggest fucking whale of a donor, and you'll never guess who it is!"

"Um..." Why was Kate sweating? There was nothing suspicious in Anna's tone. "The Queen of England?"

"Make a *real* guess."

"Uh..." Kate tried to think of some other rich Chicagoan, but her brain couldn't come up with anyone but Mikhail.

"I'll give you a hint—you *know* him."

"How would you know?"

"What?"

"What? Nothing. Uh..."

Out of patience, Anna burst out excitedly, "Mikhail Volkov!"

"Oh my gosh! Whaaaat? That's so crazy!"

Anna paused. "Why do you sound weird?"

"I don't sound weird. I'm climbing the stairs to my apartment. I'm out of breath." She wasn't—she was so used to climbing four flights of stairs every day, she could practically levitate up them at this point.

"Well, anyway, what a small world, right? The guy who saves the shelter is my friend's boss?"

"Well, he's not *really* my boss. I mean, yeah, he's the CEO, but like, my actual boss is the department head. It's not like Mikhail Volkov is personally acquainted with every Domovoy employee."

"Whatever."

Anna clearly had no interest in the details, and Kate had to forcibly restrain herself from blurting out a defensive monologue about how little connection her job had to the CEO.

"Anyways, he donated *five hundred thousand.*"

"What?" Kate came to a standstill on the landing. She'd only told him sixty thousand.

"Yeah, it's insane. His personal assistant reached out to the board with an inquiry about what was needed. When they told her they needed sixty grand to pay the mortgage for the year, she asked how much was remaining on the mortgage—and donated the lump sum, and then some!"

"Wow," Kate said faintly.

"With the extra funding, they'll be able to improve a bunch of stuff on the building, too. Jasmine nearly passed out with shock when she found out."

"Wow," Kate said again, at a loss.

"I mean, nobody needs to be *that* fucking rich," Anna said, slightly aggrieved—and Kate couldn't help but agree, "but at least he's doing good things with his money, right?"

"Yeah... um. Yeah. Definitely."

Chapter Fifteen

"If you come inside me, I'll be forced to punish you."

Mikhail had only landed in Chicago a couple of hours ago, and the first thing he'd done was call Kate. Now he was naked, seated in front of the chessboard, hands gripping the arms of his chair as if it were the only thing keeping him tethered to the earth. Kate was in the process of lowering herself onto his cock, taking him into the hot, silky clasp of her body. He felt her inner muscles stretch and flex as she sank down, pulling him in deeper and deeper.

He drew in a staggered breath. "Knyazhna, I can't—"

"Shush," she said impatiently, though a hint of breathlessness betrayed her.

Her full weight settled on his lap, his entire cock buried deep inside her perfect cunt. He spread his thighs restlessly, letting out another tortured groan as he felt her clench down on him.

She laughed at his agony. "Oops, so sorry," she said insincerely. "Now. Let's begin. You're white."

"Pawn to e4," he gritted out.

She leaned forward to move his pawn for him and the subtle movement of her body was torturously stimulating. He couldn't help himself, his hands went to her hips, gripping her over her rucked-up skirt before sliding down to her bare thighs.

"Knyazhna…"

"I don't remember saying you could touch me." She bounced a little, riding up and down his cock in slight increments.

"Ah, no. No, please—" His hands tightened on her thighs, trying to hold her in place. "Please knyazhna, you'll make me—"

She kept on bouncing. "Hands off, then."

The exquisite feeling of her pussy squeezing on him with each little bounce was making it impossible to think. The physical pleasure of the current predicament was at war with the need to obey—to not come before he had permission. He didn't want to fail. But if he failed, he'd not only get to come, he'd also have the masochistic joy of however she decided to punish him.

The urge to obey—to succeed—won out. With a pained breath, he wrenched his hands away from her thighs, gripping the arms of the chair again with white-knuckled desperation.

Kate settled her ass back onto his lap with a wicked giggle. "Good boy." After a moment, she elbowed him gently. "Your turn."

"Oh." He looked over her shoulder at the board, saw that she'd opened with her king's knight. "Knight to c3."

Her inner muscles flexed around him again as she leaned forward to make his move. He concentrated on breathing in through his nose and out through his mouth, keeping his hands securely on the arms of the chair. Kate remained in that posture for a second before deciding to move her bishop out.

Mikhail tried his damnedest to keep a clear head and play competitively. He enjoyed beating her at chess. The way a loss lit her eyes up with wounded pride and competitive frustration was viscerally beautiful. But the way she channeled that frustration into sexual physicality was nothing short of divine.

But no matter how clear he tried to keep his mind, the feeling of being inside Kate was burning through his brain cells like wildfire. He lost his queen ridiculously early in the game. He thought he'd gotten ahold of himself, but quickly lost a knight and a bishop to careless mistakes. Kate's delight was palpable—happy little squeezes on his cock every time she laughed, restless wiggling on his lap when she celebrated another capture.

She wasn't immune to the feeling, either. When she forgot herself and leaned too far forward, Mikhail knew he was hitting a sweet spot. Her choked little gasp and the sudden stillness of her whole body had him forgetting the rules—hands flying to grasp her by the hips, his own hips working instinctively to grind deep into her heat.

She didn't stop him right away. Instead, she gripped the sides of the table, head lowered, letting out shallow, panting breaths with each roll of his hips. Mikhail groaned as pleasure lanced through him, but the sound broke whatever spell had fallen over Kate.

"Stop," she said breathlessly.

The noise that came out of him was inhuman, but he

managed to make his body obey. Every muscle was drawn tight, trembling with the agony of self-denial.

"What's your next move?" she asked, voice strained.

He stared at the board, trying to make sense of it. "Rook to d5."

She slid his rook over, then reached across the board to bring out the bishop she'd left lurking in the wings.

"Checkmate," she said with quiet triumph.

He blinked. His gaze darted around the board. It took several seconds before it sank in—he'd lost. "*Blyat*," he swore softly.

She giggled. "Guess what happens now."

He had no idea. Between the feel of her pussy squeezing him and the shock of his defeat, he couldn't piece two thoughts together.

"I'm feeling generous," she purred, arching back against him. She reached up, sliding her hands around the back of his neck while her hips ground taunting circles. "You can come inside me."

It didn't seem possible, but he somehow went even more rigid. "Knyazhna," he rasped. "Don't tease."

"I'm not teasing." She bounced a little, forcing an animalistic groan from him. Her fingernails scored up and down the nape of his neck. "I beat you, and now I'm going to fuck you. You're the spoils of war. Now, make me come, and then you can have yours."

His hands were on her immediately, stroking, gripping, squeezing. His movements were almost frantic, desperate to feel every inch of her, to take full advantage of the free reign he'd been given. He half-expected to be reprimanded for his clumsy enthusiasm, but instead, Kate arched into his hands, soft moans rising in her throat as she ground down on him, her pussy squeezing his cock like a fist.

Mikhail slid one hand beneath her sweater, reaching up to grasp the soft weight of one breast through the tissue-fine lace of her bra. Her nipple was a stiff point against his palm. He stroked his thumb over it, pulling stuttering breaths from Kate, making her pussy clench harder. He slid his other hand between her thighs, gently circling two fingers over the peak of her clit.

"*Ah!* Yes—right there. Oh god. Yes."

Mikhail couldn't keep the rest of his body under control anymore. He planted his heels against the floor and worked his hips, thrusting up into her with desperate, rocking digs.

"Oh, good boy, good boy," she panted, rolling her hips with his thrusts. "Just like that. Such a good—" Kate's words were lost in a sudden cry. Her nails dug into his nape as her spine arched and her legs shook. Her pussy squeezed his cock in rolling waves, snapping through the last thread of his self-control.

Mikhail shuddered and groaned, clutching onto Kate for dear life as his climax barreled through him. Pulse after pulse of hot, all-consuming pleasure seized him, thunder and lightning in his veins, wildfire across his skin. He felt his come jetting into the hot clasp of her body, and that primal satisfaction only intensified the unbearable ecstasy.

When he came back to his senses, Kate was slumped against him, breathing raggedly, fingertips tracing restlessly over his arms. He could hold her like this forever, and never tire of it.

That thought was immediately chased by a flash of cold dread. *No*, he could *not* hold her forever. This would end. He needed it to end.

Another contradictory feeling had him tightening his hold on her, clutching her tightly against him. She was warmth and comfort and pleasure in a way that felt separate from the sex. He didn't know what to do with that feeling. Despite the warm glow, it felt threatening. Dangerous.

Kate blew out a heavy breath, pushing against the arms of the chair to sit up straight. Mikhail resisted for a second, keeping hold of her.

"Let me go," she said with a laugh.

Her playfulness only made the warm glow worse. For his own sake, he forced himself to obey, releasing her. Kate eased herself up gently. His softening cock slid free of her, leaving a trail of his come down her thigh.

Before this had even begun, Kate had provided Mikhail proof that she was on birth control—an IUD, something she couldn't forget to take. Even so, the sight of his seed dripping out of her filled him with a feral pleasure he'd never experienced before. He'd given that to her—or she'd taken it from him. If she wanted, she could secretly take out that IUD and tie them together forever. The idea of being trapped like that, by Kate, sent an unexpected lance of sharp arousal through him.

Dangerous. She was the most dangerous woman he'd ever known.

Kate *tsk*ed, drawing his attention to her flushed, bright-eyed face. Her clothes were rumpled and askew, but she was still dressed, gazing down at his naked body with an expression of amused disdain.

His cock pulsed again.

"You're a mess," she said, scorn in her voice, but a smile in her eyes.

"I know."

"I'm going to go clean up. You should, too." She started for the door.

"Let me clean you." The words came out without thought.

She paused, considering. "Alright."

He took her to the nearest guest bedroom, through to the en suite bathroom where, to his surprise, Kate stripped entirely. He watched in mute astonishment as her body was revealed in portions. First the skirt gone, then the sweater. Stockings next, then panties, finally the bra.

It was the first time he'd seen her whole body. Her pale skin was gleaming with sweat, her thighs streaked with his drying semen. Her breasts were perfect handfuls, tipped with light pink nipples. There was a small birthmark on her left hip, a slightly darker splotch of skin, shaped vaguely like a heart.

Kate crossed her arms beneath her breasts, raising her eyebrows. His silent staring had gone on too long. Jarring himself into motion, he stepped into the shower stall and got the water running. When it was warm, he ushered Kate in.

"Are you cold-blooded?" she yelped, ducking out of the spray.

"What?"

"I don't know what you're used to in Arctic Siberia—"

"I'm from Volgograd."

"—but *that* is not a hot shower."

He adjusted the temperature a few degrees upward. Kate reached a hand in and frowned. "Still no. Show me how this works. Actually, never mind, I can figure it out."

Amused, Mikhail let himself be nudged aside by her slighter form. She tapped at the control panel, pushing the temperature higher and higher.

"Katya," he objected with dismay. "You're going to boil yourself like a lobster."

She blinked at him, not responding immediately. After an odd pause, she bit her lip and turned away from him, stepping into the shower. "I like boiling myself. Come on." She held a hand out, gesturing for him to join her.

He stepped in, but paused on the periphery, hissing at the feel of liquid hot magma hitting his legs.

Kate laughed at him. "What a wimp. I'm going to have to find myself a tougher slave."

He knew she was joking, but a bolt of icy hot panic cut through his chest. He caught her around the waist, driving her against the shower wall, pinning her there with his body. Her hellfire shower rained down on his back, probably eating his skin right off his bones.

"Take it back," he demanded.

Kate gazed up at him, eyes narrowed—but not with anger. She was contemplating him. It was an oddly vulnerable sensation, and he didn't much care for it. But he remained there, his body pressed to hers, as long as she would tolerate it.

Her expression relaxed. "I wouldn't really do that," she said, speaking with such careful kindness, he almost flinched. He wanted to recoil from her, walk away, but he couldn't make his body comply.

"I know." Still, he held her, letting her astute gaze bore into him. He couldn't look away.

Several breaths passed between them, the air thick with fog, their bodies growing slick in the steam—probably from sweat because *fuck* did she like a hot shower.

Eventually, he couldn't take it anymore. He drew back, taking Kate with him, pulling her beneath the shower stream.

She closed her eyes, head tilting back to let the water coast over her face and body. Keeping one arm around her, Mikhail reached for one of the nearby bottles, uncertain whether he was grabbing shampoo or body wash or something else entirely. Whatever it was, it sudsed in his hands, and he began rubbing it over Kate's skin, working his fingers into the muscles of her shoulders and down along the sides of her spine.

She murmured something inaudible, tipping her head forward to rest her cheek against his shoulder, pliant under his touch. It felt like as much of a victory as making her come did. His cock took notice, but the feeling wasn't sexual, really. He couldn't identify it.

She murmured again and this time Mikhail asked, "Hm?"

"Didn't want to get my hair wet," she said. "Oh well."

The sleepiness in her voice and the trusting wrap of her arms around his waist exacerbated that weird feeling. That same chest pressure he'd felt on the plane was back. He couldn't have a heart attack right now—he was too busy seeing to his printsessa. He pressed his palm to his sternum, willing it away. Guiding Kate to sit on the tiled bench, he crouched before her and soaped up her legs, taking care to rinse sticky come and sweat from between her thighs. He worked his way down to her feet, pressing his thumbs into her arches, drawing delicious moans from her.

When she was rinsed and clean, Mikhail turned to step out of the shower, to fetch her a towel, but she caught his wrist and dragged him back, pushing him to sit on the bench she'd just vacated.

"Katya—" he objected.

Her gaze lit on his and held for a moment. And then he heard it—realized what he'd done.

"Knyazhna, I meant," he corrected himself.

Kate shrugged, smiling. "You can call me Katya. I like it."

"Better than 'knyazhna'?"

"No. I like 'knyazhna' when you're serving me. But when we're just... just ourselves, you can call me Katya."

"Hmm. Katya."

She gave him another smile, then poured soap into her hands and began working it over his body. He forgot why he'd tried to stop her. Her hands, as he well knew, were strong. But this was the first time she'd turned that strength so gently on him. She massaged his chest and shoulders. She worked her way down his arms and then his thighs with firm, kneading pressure. He hadn't realized how tightly he held himself until his muscles began to relax under her hands.

When she was done, he stood and rinsed beneath the scorching hot water.

"Alright, now prepare yourself."

"For what?"

"This is how I like to finish a shower." She tapped at the control panel, aggressively lowering the water temperature until Mikhail yelped like a kicked puppy. Molten lava turned to daggers of ice within seconds.

"You are insane," he gasped, dodging from beneath the cold spray.

"No, come back!" She laughed, hugging herself and shivering as the water ran over her body.

"Not on pain of death." Mikhail reached for a towel.

"You have to! If you don't stand under the cold water for a bit, you'll start sweating while you dry off, which defeats the whole purpose of taking a shower."

"Sweating is good for the body." This hot and cold shower reminded him vaguely of Russian banyas, though he'd never much visited them. A common cultural touchpoint, lost on him because impoverished orphans did not have access to such things. Any resentment he felt was old and stale, long forgotten. His only objection now was to the physical unpleasantness of the task.

"Not if it dries on your skin."

"I would rather be covered in dry sweat than have my testicles retract entirely inside my body."

She laughed again. She was beginning to shiver, teeth chattering as she smiled at him.

"Come on, Katya, get out. You'll freeze."

Her smile turned impish. "I'm not getting out until you come in."

Muttering curses, Mikhail took a breath and stepped back under the freezing spray. She was right—he was sheened with sweat from the heat of the shower. And while the cold water was an unpleasant shock, it did rinse him clean and cool the hot flush beneath his skin.

"Can we get out now?" he pleaded, cupping his groin protectively.

"I suppose." She let him turn off the water, then stood patiently while he toweled her off. Mikhail helped her pull her clothing back on.

"Give me another game of chess," he said as he pulled up the zipper on her skirt.

"Alright."

BACK IN THE STUDY, MIKHAIL PULLED HIS PANTS ON while Kate took a seat at the chessboard, setting their pieces back up—Mikhail as white, herself as black. He sat across from her, bare-chested, still damp from the shower. That medal glinted against his chest hair, calling her attention. She'd asked about it weeks ago, and he'd been terse, but the damn thing was getting harder and harder to ignore. He *always* wore it. Always.

Mikhail opened with his king's knight, dragging her attention back to the game. Kate opened with her queen's pawn, and they were off.

"How was Shanghai? And Tokyo?" Kate asked as he considered his next move.

"Better than usual." He moved his bishop out to midboard.

"How so?" That bishop had two potential paths, one threatening her knight, the other her rook. Kate's eyes traced over the board, trying to figure out how to neutralize his bishop or, failing that, which piece she was most willing to sacrifice.

"I saw much more of Shanghai than I normally do. It's usually just boardrooms and hotels and restaurants and smog. But I went into the markets to get your pictures."

Kate's gaze lifted to his briefly. He'd enjoyed his trip better because of *her?* "Oh." She looked back down at the board, reaching for one of her pawns. "Well, I liked the pictures. I'll probably never get to see Shanghai in person."

"I'll take you."

Her fingers froze on the pawn. She looked up at him again. "What?"

"I'll take you to Shanghai."

"What?"

Mikhail frowned. "Am I not speaking English?"

"No, you are. I just— I can't even— You'll take me to *Shanghai?*"

"Would you rather go somewhere else?"

She stared blankly at him.

"Where would you go?" he pressed. "If you could go anywhere?"

Kate shook her head, absently sliding the pawn forward. "I don't know. I've never left the country. I don't even have a passport." She couldn't afford it.

"Get a passport." He slid his bishop over to capture her rook. "Apply for expedited processing."

"I've already planned all my vacation days this year. I don't have any PTO left."

Mikhail shrugged. "I'll arrange it."

"If you intervene to get me more time off, HR is going to know that something's going on between us."

Mikhail looked up at her with a wolfish twinkle in his eye. "Katya, I own the fucking company. What is HR going to do to me?"

Kate was simultaneously charmed by his irreverence, and annoyed by his obtuseness. "I don't care what they do about *you*—I care about *me*. How am I supposed to keep working with all these people when they're whispering behind my back about how I'm fucking the boss?"

He shrugged again, unconcerned. "Then don't work with them. I could take care of you."

That was the second time he'd brought up the idea of her leaving her job and becoming his... what, exactly? She was afraid of the answer. So she changed the subject.

"When I was a little kid I was obsessed with Machu Picchu."

One Saturday morning, she and Angel had been quietly

watching PBS kids' shows while their dad slept off his hangover. One of those short, educational bits in between commercials had been all about Machu Picchu, and both she and Angel had been fascinated.

They'd invented a game where the couch, recliner, and coffee table were the Inca Trail—and then been reamed out by their dad when he caught them climbing on the furniture. At school, the librarian had helped them find all the books the school library had about Machu Picchu, and llamas, and Peru, and the Inca. She and Angel had taken turns checking them out over and over again, poring over them, playing pretend games where they lived in the ancient citadel as powerful priestesses.

In the years since then, Kate had almost entirely forgotten about it. She wondered if Angel remembered.

"I've never been there," Mikhail said. "Would you like to go?"

Kate avoided answering, pretending to debate her next move, even though she knew exactly what she wanted to do. Finally, she moved her knight. "With your wealth, I would've expected you've seen the whole world."

He rested his chin in his hand as he considered the board. "No. Until I emigrated to the U.S., I'd never left Russia. Until I started Domovoy, I never left the U.S. Now I travel all the time, but mostly to industrial cities and technology centers. Silicon Valley. Geneva. Hsinchu. Dubai."

"Don't you take vacations?"

He castled his king. "Yes. To the usual places."

"I think your 'usual' places are probably different from mine."

"Where do you vacation, then?"

Kate moved her queen out to take one of his knights. "I

don't know... the exotic shores of Lake Michigan? A few years ago I was feeling *really* adventurous, and I went on a road trip to Yellowstone." It was the furthest she'd ever been from home. "You probably go to, like, Fiji. And Tahoe. And Paris."

Mikhail smiled ruefully. "I have been to all of those places." He paused for a moment, seeming to consider the board. "Get your passport, knyazhna," he said quietly.

Soft warmth moved through her veins like syrup. She loved the honorific he'd bestowed upon her. She wished she had something equivalent for him. "Slave" felt too harsh. "Pet" was close, but not quite right. He was a big, powerful, dangerous man, who submitted only to her. He was like a snarling wolf that had allowed itself to be tamed by one person—*her*. If she'd had a real wolf, she wouldn't call him "pet." She'd call him by his name. But Mikhail was a CEO's name, not a pet wolf's. Something more intimate would suit, but all she could think of was "Mike," which sounded ridiculous. She fought a smile as she considered calling him that, just to see his reaction.

"Do you always go by Mikhail?" she asked.

"People often call me 'Mr. Volkov'."

"Well, I'm not going to call you that. Is there a short form for Mikhail?"

"Misha. Or even Mishka, though that one's more... familiar."

"Mishka?" She tilted her head, considering him. "You could be my Mishka."

Something unreadable crossed his face. She was getting to know his tells, though. She suspected he was pleased.

"Yes, that'll do," she concluded. "Mishka."

He stared at her, saying nothing. But warmth gleamed in his eyes as he regarded her across the chessboard.

Oof. That look was giving her *feelings*. She bit her lips to keep from smiling at him like a lovestruck puppy. "Your turn," she prompted.

He blinked, returning his attention to the board. Just like that, the moment was gone. But the echo of it lingered, making Kate feel snug and warm, ensconced in the quiet of his study, so absorbed in their game, they could have been the only two people in the world.

Chapter Sixteen

With each passing day, Mikhail found himself carving more and more time out of his schedule for Kate. Time he would have previously spent poring over reports, projections, and analytics was being shunted to the side so that he could feed his addiction. He'd never been so ruled by his libido. In the past, these arrangements had been like scratching an itch—he needed relief, he got some, he went on with his life. But this time, each meeting only inflamed him more. She was like a drug, and the more he used, the more he needed.

It would end. All things did. Endings were an inevitable consequence of any beginning. Mikhail had learned that lesson more thoroughly than most people had to. But that didn't mean he was wrong. His childhood and early adulthood had been a string of severed relationships. He'd been born and immediately abandoned. Raised in orphanages where caretakers came and went. When he showed early academic talent, he was shuffled first to one boarding school, then to another, so any friendships he developed were inherently temporary.

As a young man, he'd chosen to go to the US for grad school, where he ended up immigrating entirely, cutting off all ties with his fatherland and anybody he knew there. As a computer engineer and businessman, he'd learned to never get attached to ideas, people, or places—it was what allowed him to rise to his current position. The only things that had any permanence were those things that Mikhail had created himself—his patents, his company, and the life he had built off of them. Everything else was tenuous and ephemeral. He could guarantee only himself.

And now, the idea of growing close to Kate was both terrifying and painful, because the loss of that connection was inevitable, and he was tired of the pain. People said it was better to have loved and lost than to have never loved at all, but Mikhail felt certain that those people had only lost once or twice. Not over and over and over again. Because, at a certain point, there was no point getting attached to anything that you knew would be taken from you.

And maybe there was no point in indulging his need for the way Kate made him feel, because he hadn't even lost her yet, and already the looming certainty of it was making him crazed. He needed her all the time. He had to resist the urge, a hundred times a day, to go see her at her desk. His home felt empty without her. He wanted to call her over constantly, not just for sex, but for a few games of chess. He wanted to buy her things, not because he wanted the gratification of submitting to her, but because he wanted to make her smile.

All of which made the inevitable demise of their arrangement that much more distressing. He knew, logically, that when his interest died out, so too would the fear of losing her. And even so, he lived in dread of that day. Until then, he savored every drop of pleasure, every ounce of ecstasy, and every moment of the strange, quiet contentment he felt with her, hoarding them up as a bulwark against the empty, stretching hollowness he felt when he thought of their eventual parting of ways.

He reveled in debasing himself for her, suffering for her, whether she punished him through humiliation, pain, or denial. He found salvation in serving her, in earning the rewards she doled out with such unrestrained, playful joy. He'd heard this called "play" before, but with Kate, it was the first time it felt like any such thing. Before meeting her, it had been a primal need that he fulfilled like any other. He ate when he was hungry, he slept when he was tired, and he found a woman to submit to when he was horny. But his wicked, capricious, sensual Katya, his knyazhna, had ripped the rug out from under him and turned what should have been a straightforward transaction into something deeper. Sometimes, it terrified him how desperately he needed her. But then he would see her again, be with her, and the fear was forgotten in the joy of her company.

There was no room for fear when he was stripped bare, kneeling at her command, crawling for her pleasure, begging for her mercy. With Kate, he could let go of everything—every unwanted feeling, every dark thought—and simply obey. And then when she'd wrung every possible bit of pleasure out of him, used him for her own ends, and then potentially deigned to allow him the ecstasy of release, there was still no room for any doubt or regret because she was still with him as he came down from the high, seated across the chessboard, amusing him with her competitive surliness.

Playing chess against her was a bit like swimming through a school of piranhas. She attacked so aggressively from so many different angles, attempting to blitz her opponent into confusion until she could find an opening to set up checkmate. Luckily for Mikhail, he was a patient, almost sedate, player. He enjoyed the challenge of parrying her many attacks, focusing on defense while quietly slipping in for the checkmate, like an assassin in the night.

What he enjoyed even more, contrary to his nature, were the conversations they had over the board, growing in intimacy with each passing day.

"Why Chicago?" Kate asked one night, running her fingers through her hair over and over again, a repetitive behavior he'd noticed from her before. "Why not Silicon Valley or Seattle or one of the bigger tech hubs?"

Mikhail watched her continue to comb at her hair. It was obviously clear of snarls, but she kept feeling along individual strands of hair, seemingly oblivious that she was doing it.

"Why do you do that to your hair?" he asked.

She snatched her hand away, looking mildly embarrassed. "I asked you a question first," she said defensively.

"I chose Chicago because of a non-compete clause I'd signed with my former employer. I'd lived and worked in San Jose before starting Domovoy. And Chicago's a big enough city, with enough tech workers, that I knew I'd have my pick of a crop of computer engineers and software developers who were hungry for exciting work, but unable to make it to the coasts, for whatever reason."

"Hmm. Mercenary."

He shrugged. "It's a business. Now my question. Why do you fiddle with your hair so much?"

She hesitated, looking down at the board. It was her turn, but she didn't seem to be contemplating her move. Without looking up at him, she said, "When I was a kid, my parents didn't take care of us very well. I had to have my head shaved twice because of mats in my hair, and I got lice, like, once a year until I was old enough to figure out how to take care of myself. It's just a habit now, to always be checking my hair."

Mikhail was speechless. He hadn't expected a confession like that. He'd expected her to say that she liked the feel of smooth hair, or something equally inconsequential. Something inside his chest drew tight, like a spring about to snap from the tension.

"Ah, Katya," he said heavily. "I didn't know."

She huffed out a breath, almost a laugh, but without any humor behind it. "Well, you wouldn't. I've made damn sure people don't see that in me anymore."

"I'm familiar with lice," Mikhail said quietly, needing to soothe her obvious discomfort. It was something he'd never spoken of since leaving Russia. "Lice infestations run through orphanages like wildfire."

Kate lifted her gaze to his, eyes wide with surprise. "Orphanages?"

Another topic he never discussed. "Yes. You knew I didn't know my parents."

"I knew you didn't know your father. But your mother, too? I... I'm sorry. That's..." She shook her head, at a loss. "Did you ever know her?"

"No. I was left in a church as a newborn."

Kate's gaze dropped to the Marian medallion hanging from his neck. She opened her mouth, about to speak, but Mikhail cut in before she could even begin.

"It is what it is," he said flatly. He nodded at the chess-board. "Your turn."

She took the hint, abandoning the painful conversation to focus on the game. The coil in his chest twisted tighter.

He couldn't explain to himself why he'd told her all of that. He wasn't a monster, he was capable of empathy. But he'd never felt the urge to bare his own vulnerabilities to smooth over someone else's. Kate was unraveling him in so many ways. He had to be careful that he wasn't completely undone by the end of their time together. He had to guard himself. It was the only way to survive.

Chapter Seventeen

Despite his resolve to be more guarded, it was impossible with Kate.

He was sprawled across the surface of his desk, bare ass pressed to smooth wood, hauling in ragged gasps of air as he came down from the sensory overload she'd just put him through. She was draped atop him, catching her own breath, face buried in his neck. Her fingertips ran in slow trails up and down his arms, an absent gesture that she seemed to need as much as he needed to feel it.

He'd never allowed this sort of thing before. Once the sex was over, intimacies were unwelcome until he felt the urge again. But he couldn't tell Kate to stop, couldn't ask her to leave. He mentally recoiled from the thought of doing so.

"I knew you had a talented mouth," Kate murmured against the sensitive skin of his neck. "But I've really been missing out on that cock."

He grunted indistinctly, still a little dizzy from the force of the orgasm that had thundered through him. He'd certainly been ridden before, but he'd never had a woman do so after shoving him onto his own desk and gagging him with a crumpled-up expense report.

After making him remove every piece of her clothing with his mouth only, she'd caught him unawares, hooking her foot behind his knee and using his own mass against him. He'd nearly cracked his head open on the mahogany surface, but all in all, he considered the potential brain injury a fair price for the blissful mind-obliterating pleasure that had followed. She liked to tease him, his vicious knyazhna, to draw out his anticipation and need until he was nothing but a hammering pulse and raw nerve endings. But when she finally let him come, the release was greater than any he'd ever felt before.

He lifted his head as Kate slid off of him. She combed at her hair, caught Mikhail watching her do it, and snatched her hand away.

He sat up. "Your hair is perfect, Katya."

"I know, I just... I have to check." A faint blush touched her cheeks, and she looked away from him.

He couldn't have that. "I still hide food," he said.

"What?"

He wished he hadn't spoken, but it was too late now. "I still hide food. When I was a child, there was never enough. When there were scraps to steal, I'd hide what I could—usually bread, but sometimes packaged things."

"You still do that?"

He nodded. "Sealed packages only. And always in... understandable places. Desk drawers. End tables."

"Do you have any hidden in here?"

"Yes." The bottom, left-side drawer. A jar of roasted peanuts, hidden behind several files. He had no intention of ever eating them. He had plenty of food in his kitchen. He could eat at the finest of restaurants whenever he wished. He just felt better knowing they were there.

"Well, then you can't judge me for picking at my hair." She immediately resumed combing her fingers through it, looking both defiant and fragile.

"I would never judge you for that."

Her expression softened, and her hand fell away from the nape of her neck. After a moment's pause, she said, "I'm going to shower."

"I'll wash you." He got up to follow her.

"Alright, but don't get my hair wet this time."

———

KATE WAS IN TROUBLE. *FEELINGS* WERE STARTING TO SET in. Or maybe they'd been setting in for a long time now and were finally reaching the threshold where her emotionally stunted brain could actually recognize them. She had thousands of dollars in clothes and jewelry and technical gadgets that filled her with a soft golden warmth that had nothing to do with their actual cost or social cachet, but with the irrational sense of safety they imparted. Some days, she just stood in front of her open closet door, admiring the beautiful clothing hanging neatly in a row. The only thing that didn't give her that feeling was the dutch oven. Every time she tried to use it, she was overwhelmed by the same choking weepiness that had embarrassed her a month ago on Michigan Ave.

And Mikhail kept making it worse. It wasn't even the money. Kate wasn't used to being taken care of, and he kept doing little things, things he didn't even seem to be aware of. Like reaching over to cover the corner of the table when Kate ducked down to retrieve a fallen chess piece so that she didn't hit her head on it when she sat back up. Or zipping her dress up for her, even after they'd slipped out of the dynamic. Or gently combing his fingers through her hair after sex, assuring her there were no tangles. Or memorizing the exact temperature she liked the shower set to, and stoically enduring it every time.

And listening to her. Just listening, and actually hearing her, and caring about what she had to say. Even on topics she really had no business opining on to the billionaire who was paying her for sex—like capitalism and corporate greed.

"You don't think I should *exist?*" Mikhail echoed, amused.

Kate bit her lip, regretting the words immediately. She'd gotten too comfortable talking to him about anything and everything—favorite TV shows, current events, their shitty childhoods—and had somehow gotten on a roll about poverty and wealth hoarding, and had accidentally blurted out words that, while true, probably were best left unsaid in certain kinds of company. Like the company of actual fucking billionaires.

"I think *you*, Mikhail Volkov, the human being, have every right to exist. But nobody deserves your level of wealth, especially when so many people around the world have nothing. Hundreds of millions is already excessive. More than a billion is absurd."

Mikhail rested his chin on his hand, their chess game momentarily forgotten as he considered her, interest and amusement both gleaming in his dark eyes. "So what do you propose, then?"

"*Way* higher wealth taxes. Higher taxes on capital gains. Taxes on unrealized gains."

The amused glimmer in his eyes faded. He wasn't angry

or offended, just quietly intent. "How would I pay taxes on unrealized gains, when they exceed the value of my liquid assets?"

"Divest your investments." She shrugged.

"So I should give up my shares of the company I created in order to pay tax on value that only exists in theory?"

"Everything about money only exists in theory. Currency only has value because we've all agreed to the collective delusion that it does. Your 'theoretical' money has the same power as 'real' money."

Mikhail tilted his head as he considered that. "I can't say that you're entirely wrong," he conceded. "But I don't see why I should pay the price for a faulty system. I'm not a trust-fund brat living off of generational wealth. I built my own company with my own skills and knowledge. I had nothing—*nothing*—to my name, and I was an immigrant on top of it."

"You had a scholarship to attend school in the U.S., and you were able to immigrate here because schools and workplaces sponsored your visas."

"Yes, because I had a skill they wanted. It wasn't a gift, Katya. They were using me to their advantage, just as I used them."

"Those are still advantages that most people don't have. Your aptitude for computer science is an advantage. Not everybody has it—not everybody *can* have it. People have different natural talents and interests. Some people are innately drawn to botany, or art, or teaching. But wealthy countries aren't falling over themselves to recruit great teachers, even though they're invaluable to society."

"This is true," Mikhail acknowledged, gripping his Marian medallion, thumb stroking pensively over the worn surface. "So what would you have me do, then? Sell my ownership of Domovoy? What does that do to balance the scales? Nothing."

"That's not what I'm saying."

"Then what, Katya? What can I, personally, do to alleviate the unfairness of a system I did not build?"

Kate realized she was sweating. How had she gotten into this conversation? Why couldn't she shut herself up?

"Put your financial support behind legislation that fixes injustices and politicians who'll pass it. Throw your money at charities that alleviate systemic suffering. Hell, if you just instituted some sort of profit-sharing program at the company, you'd go a long way in changing a lot of people's lives for the better—and making sure workers are reaping the actual dividends of their labor."

Mikhail's dark eyes glittered as he regarded her across the chessboard. "It sounds like an American is lecturing a Russian about communism."

"Oh, please," Kate scoffed. "You were like, eight years old when the Soviet Union collapsed. And you're American now, too. And the Soviet Union wasn't even actually communist."

Mikhail tilted his head, considering her. "It sounds like you know a lot about it," he said skeptically.

"All I know is I grew up with *nothing*, and it sucked. Childhood should be fun, but mine was awful. If people who have too much—you know, *billionaires*—could spread the wealth around a little bit, fewer kids would have to live in those conditions."

"Don't lecture me about poverty. I had even less than you," Mikhail said heatedly.

"Then you should understand! You should want to make it so nobody else has to go through that!"

"Why do *I* have to care, when nobody else does? Why is this on my shoulders?"

"Because you have the means! If *I* had your money, it'd be on *me*."

"You want one person to fill the role that governments should be filling. That sounds precarious."

"I don't want one person to do it. I want a better system, but for a better system to happen, the people with the most power have to make it happen."

Mikhail was quiet, looking down at the board as he took that in. Kate's heart thundered in her chest. After a moment, his gaze lifted to Kate's, and all the hectic uncertainty seemed to die away. There was only the heavy, dark pin of his gaze.

"You have all the power here, knyazhna."

She didn't know what to say. How could he not understand that his money meant he'd always have the power in their relationship? Or was she the one who was misunderstanding?

Chapter Eighteen

He wasn't sure why being told he didn't deserve the wealth he'd built should flood him with arousal and play on endless repeat in his brain, but Kate's sorcery had done its work, and it was all he could think of. It wasn't that he was turned on by the idea of losing his wealth. It was more that she'd presented him with a challenge—*convince me you deserve your wealth*—and that challenge fired his blood and obsessed his mind. He would convince her. It was easy to criticize from the sidelines—but if she actually had skin in the game? She wouldn't be so dismissive.

It was time to present his proposition.

After he'd brought up creating a position for Kate, his personal assistant had come back to him with a list of potential job titles. *Social Coordinator. Domestic Assistant. Travel Attendant.* Any of them would work. He'd offer a seven-figure salary and a benefits package that would make her faint, and then he'd claim his victory on his knees, with Kate where she belonged—with him, over him, always.

Always?

He brushed that uncomfortable thought away. It would last as long as it was meant to, though he couldn't deny he had expectations that exceeded past experiences.

Monday morning, his self-control was shot. He'd intended to have her over after work and make the offer then. He'd only been at the office for an hour when he gave in and asked one of the office assistants to have Kate Pasternak sent up to his office.

A few minutes later, a message pinged to his computer. *Kate Pasternak is out sick today. Would you like to speak to one of the logistics managers, or someone else in the department?*

Mikhail frowned as he re-read the message. Sick?

No, he replied. *It can wait.*

He pulled out his phone and immediately called Kate. After several rings, it went to voicemail. Perturbed, he texted her:

> Are you Ill?

He stared at his phone, waiting. When she didn't immediately reply, he got up, pacing restlessly to the windows. He stared out at the city, looked back down at his phone, then back out the windows again. Several agitated minutes passed before he brought his phone back up to call her again.

Before he got that far, her response came in via text.

> I'm fine. Just a little run down.

> Have you gone to the doctor?

I don't need to go to the doctor. They'll just
tell me it's a virus and that I should drink lots
of fluids and rest.

Do you have lots of fluids?

Well, I've been fortunate enough to land an
apartment with indoor plumbing, so yes.

Her sarcasm reassured him, but there was still a tight
band squeezing around his chest.

Do you have somebody who can look
after you?

It's just a cold. I don't need looking after.

Do you have somebody?

Yes, mother. I have a roommate.

That eased his mind somewhat, but not totally.

I'm going to have food and medicine
delivered to your address.

I have food and medicine. Stop fussing. I'll
be back on my feet by tomorrow.

But she wasn't back on her feet. The next day, Mikhail
checked on her first thing, only to find out she'd called in sick
again. He closed his office door and called her. She didn't
answer. He called her again. Still no answer. Punching at his
phone screen impatiently, he texted her.

> Have you gone to the doctor?

> I was trying to sleep. Why are you blowing up my phone?

> If you're still sick, you need to go to the doctor.

> No I don't.

Mikhail fought the impulse to chuck his phone across the office. He had no way of making her go to the doctor. He couldn't stop envisioning her weak and helpless, falling into a feverish coma and slipping away on a breath. He'd seen it happen. Two different boys he'd known in the orphanage had died from fevers.

> Are you running a fever?

> A mild one. Seriously, I'm fine.

KATE HAD SLIPPED BACK INTO A FITFUL NAP, STRETCHED out on the couch while *The Price is Right* played, an array of cups and tissues and packets of cold medicine scattered across the coffee table. Suddenly, a jarring buzz filled the apartment, and she nearly leapt out of her skin. Heart pounding, she stared at the source of the noise with wide-eyed alarm, still trying to gather her fever-addled thoughts.

It was the intercom, she realized after a foggy beat. Groaning, she hauled herself upright, keeping the blanket clutched around her like a cloak. She lurched over to the intercom, moving like she'd just been hit by a truck. All of her joints ached. It hurt to breathe.

"Hello?" she rasped against the speaker.

"Katya? Let me in."

Kate blinked. That deep voice sounded like...

"Mikhail?"

"Yes. Let me in. I have food for you. And medicine."

She didn't bother pointing out that she already had food and medicine. She was too confused by his presence in the first place and too tired to argue. She pressed the button to let him in, then slumped against the wall while she waited for him to reach her door. She might have dozed off because, quite suddenly, she was startled by the sound of a heavy fist pounding on her door.

She pulled it open and found herself face to face with Mikhail. He was still dressed for work in a perfectly tailored charcoal-gray suit, but his arms were loaded down with shopping bags.

"Ah, Katya." He frowned, cupping her cheek, then feeling her forehead. "You look like death."

"Thank you," she said dryly, turning away from him and slumping her way back to the couch to sprawl gracelessly across it.

Mikhail shut the door and locked it before following her, sitting restlessly on the edge of the cushion next to her hip. He settled his bags on the coffee table and began digging through them.

"It's very difficult to find mustard compresses in American pharmacies."

"Yeah, I've always thought so too."

"But there is a Ukrainian shop near here that sells them."

"Oh, thank goodness."

"Here." He pulled out a box of something labeled with Cyrillic letters. "Let me put one on your chest."

Kate sighed, a crackling, ragged sound. "I already took some cold medicine."

Mikhail picked up the box. "*This?*" he asked dubiously.

"Yeah."

"Hm." He set it back down, then resumed opening the mustard compress. "Lift your shirt."

Amused, exhausted, Kate gave in. She pulled the hem of her shirt up to her collarbones. She wasn't wearing a bra, and she'd expected Mikhail to make some kind of comment about her bare breasts, but his gaze only traveled clinically over her exposed flesh, focusing on the portion of her chest where he carefully applied the compress. Then, very gently, he pulled her shirt back down and her blanket back up.

"Rest," he commanded, getting up from the couch. "I will make you tea. When did you last eat?"

"I don't like tea. And I don't know."

"Tea is good for fevers," he said, fishing more supplies out of his bags. He pulled out a clear take-out container filled with chicken soup. The bright yellow broth was dotted with oil, and speckled with herbs. Hearty chunks of chicken and thickly cut vegetables floated at the top. "Sit up, if you can."

"I don't want to," Kate grumbled.

"Then I will feed this to you." He started to pry the lid off.

"I can feed myself," she said quickly, pushing herself up on weak arms.

Mikhail handed her the soup and a plastic spoon. He scooped up some other supplies and went to her kitchen. Kate could see him through the wide doorway, rummaging around as if he owned the place.

"Where is your kettle, Katya?"

"I don't have one."

Mikhail dug around some more until he found a dinged-up old saucepan. He moved to the sink, filling it with water, and brought it to the stove. Kate watched him with a detached, fuzzy sort of interest. The compress on her chest was tingly and warm, a bit like menthol, but somehow smelled worse. Resigned to her fate, she started eating the soup he'd brought.

It was delicious. And her stomach, which had gone somewhat dormant in the face of all her other body pains, suddenly made a dramatic gurgling noise. It quieted down as she continued eating, and when she was done with the soup, Mikhail appeared with a steaming mug.

"Hot tea with honey and orange and spices," he pronounced, handing the mug to her. "Drink it all."

"You're really bossy when I'm not fucking you," Kate observed.

Mikhail shot her a look that was mildly exasperated, but also slightly heated. "I'm not bossy, I'm sensible. Let me look at the compress."

Kate held the warm mug between her cold hands and sat complacently while Mikhail lifted her shirt. He peeled the compress back a bit, considered it for a second, then pressed it back down.

"A few more minutes," he told her, lowering her shirt.

Kate sipped cautiously at the tea, prepared to hate it. "Oh," she said, surprised at the flavor.

"Good?"

"I mean... it doesn't really taste like tea. It tastes like hot, spicy orange juice." She paused. "That sounds like it would be gross, but it's not."

"I know. Drink it all."

Kate shrugged and did as she was told. She stared vacantly at the TV while she drank, only vaguely aware of Mikhail cleaning things up in the kitchen and rustling around in the bags he'd brought. When the mug was empty, she set it on the coffee table. Mikhail sank down next to her again, gently lifting her shirt to examine the compress once more. Her skin felt hot and tingly underneath it, and when he peeled it away, the open air felt shockingly cold against it.

"That's enough for now." He disposed of the used compress in an empty bag. "You should sleep in your bed. You can't get good rest on a sofa."

"I can't fall asleep at night if I spend the whole day in my bed."

Mikhail considered that, then relented. "Fine. Lay down, then. I'll close the curtains in here."

"Why are you doing all this?" Kate asked, sinking back down.

Mikhail paused, halfway through closing the nearest curtain panel. "You're my knyazhna," he answered flatly.

That didn't sound like the whole truth, but sleep was already tugging Kate under. She yawned and pulled her blanket up, giving in.

WHEN KATE WOKE, THE TV HAD BEEN TURNED OFF AND the apartment was completely dark except for a single lamp in the opposite corner of the room. Mikhail was seated in the armchair near her head, silently tapping away at his phone. He'd pulled off his suit coat and rolled his sleeves up to his elbows, exposing strong forearms. Kate watched him for a moment, entranced by the movement of muscle and tendons as he typed.

After a moment, his gaze flicked over to her. When he realized her eyes were open, he quickly leaned forward, setting his phone aside.

"How do you feel?" he asked, reaching out to lay his hand against her forehead. She tried to recoil—her skin was probably slicked with grease and sweat, and she hadn't showered since Sunday night. There was nowhere to go, though, and Mikhail's palm rested there for a moment, his expression thoughtful, but not disgusted.

"A little better, I think."

He nodded. "You are not so warm. Do you have a thermometer?"

She reluctantly allowed him to take her temperature, recognizing that resistance was futile.

"Hm. Ninety-nine-point-five."

"That's better than it was. I've been sitting at a hundred and two for the last day or so."

A satisfied smile quirked one corner of his mouth. "I told you, tea is good for fevers."

"It was probably the cold medicine I've been taking."

"The cold medicine that didn't do anything until after you had tea and a mustard compress?"

Kate narrowed her eyes at him. He smirked. Slowly, both their expressions shifted into genuine smiles. Abashed, Kate looked away from him, shifting herself to sit up.

"What time is it?" she asked.

"Just past six."

"Did you spend all day here?"

"Yes." His gaze tracked over her. "You are looking better, Katya. Your color is coming back."

"Must've been all the mustard." She stretched, surprised by how much less her joints ached.

"I will make more tea and heat up the soup."

"There's more soup?"

"Yes. I brought several."

After Kate had eaten and had more tea, she was genuinely feeling better. She wasn't sure she believed that mustard and hot orange juice had cured her, but she wasn't confident enough to argue against Mikhail's broody caretaking.

"Tired?" Mikhail asked as he cleared away the empty mug and bowl.

"No. Not yet."

"Would you like a game of chess?"

Kate scowled at him. "You always win, even when I'm healthy. Right now, my head's all buzzy with cold medicine. You'd beat me like a drum."

Mikhail grinned. "We'll even the odds. I'll play blindfolded."

Kate didn't answer right away. She was still too run down to be entertaining any thoughts of sex, but she couldn't deny the little frisson of *interest* at the idea of blindfolding him.

Mikhail apparently read it in her gaze, because he shook his head. "You need your strength, knyazhna. One game of chess?"

"If you're going to be blindfolded, then yes. I've never seen anyone play without seeing the board."

"I'm not very good at it. Where is your chessboard?"

He fetched it from the hall closet—a cheap little wooden box that unfolded to form the board, all the pieces contained inside when it was closed. It was nothing compared to the gorgeous marble set in Mikhail's study.

He flipped the board open on the coffee table and began setting the pieces up. When everything was in place, he pulled his necktie loose and tied it over his eyes. That little zing of excitement chased over Kate's skin again, and she bit her lip on a wolfish smile.

"Ready?" Mikhail asked.

"Yes. You first."

"Pawn to d4."

Kate moved his piece for him, then her own. They played like that, slowly, Mikhail making halting declarations for each move, growing more and more uncertain as the game progressed.

"Bishop to g7," he said slowly, still thinking on it even as he spoke.

"You can't move your bishop there, your knight's in the way."

He swore softly in Russian. "Queen to g7...?"

"That one you can do." She slid his queen forward.

The game progressed quickly, and Kate won. Mikhail pulled up the blindfold, stared at the board, and swore again.

"Another?" Kate offered, stifling a yawn. "This time without a blindfold?"

Mikhail looked over at her, thoughtful and serious. He leaned in close, cupping her cheek as his gaze tracked over her face. "You're tired again. You need to get some real sleep."

She *was* tired, but she didn't want him to leave. The dangerous feelings that had been growing for a while now had officially become a full-blown disaster. She liked him as more than just a source of ready cash and orgasms. She liked his dry humor and his protectiveness and his even his unreadable stoicism. She liked that she felt safe with him, but also unstoppably powerful. Selfishly, she liked that he wanted to give her things, and that he did so without an ounce of prickish entitlement.

She liked him too much. She was afraid it might be more than mere liking. But she was slightly comforted by the fact that he seemed to be in the same boat. What kind of detached, only-in-it-for-the-sex kind of man would leave work to make tea for his sick sex-contractor, and then sit beside her while she slept for several hours?

"Let's get you into bed," Mikhail said, reaching to help her up.

"Okay," Kate said, stupefied into agreeability by the terrifying emotional realization she was going through.

In the bedroom, Mikhail peeled her covers back and then flipped them over her once she'd crawled in. He'd brought her water bottle from the living room and set it on her nightstand. He pressed his hand to her forehead one more time, then her cheek, then the side of her neck, brow furrowed in concentration.

"Where's that thermometer?" he muttered, darting back out to the living room. He returned a second later to take her temperature. Ninety-nine-point-one. Practically normal again. Mikhail visibly relaxed at the reading, setting the thermometer on the nightstand.

"Thank you for... everything," Kate said softly.

Mikhail nodded. "If you wake up feeling too hot, or too cold, take your temperature again. If it's high, you go to a doctor."

"I'm not wracking up emergency room charges for a mild fever," she objected.

"Fevers can be deadly," Mikhail said roughly. There was

something in his gaze that told her not to argue—something fragile and dark.

"Okay," she agreed, just to put his mind at ease. "I will."

He nodded. "Good, then." He shifted restlessly at her bedside, looking cagey and uncertain. After a moment, he ducked down, pressing his lips to the top of her head. "Sleep well, Katya. Don't come into work tomorrow. Spend the day recovering."

Kate stared up at him, stunned into silence. The place where his lips had touched the crown of her head still felt the ghost of that pressure—a gentle comfort that was spreading through the rest of her body like a soft glow.

"Good," Mikhail said as if she'd agreed with him. He clicked off her bedside lamp. "Goodnight, knyazhna."

And then he was gone.

Kate lay in the dark, staring up at the ceiling, overwhelmed again by those dangerous feelings. Soft, hot tears tracked from her eyes to her temples, sliding into her hair. She didn't fight them this time. She let out a slow, shuddering breath, and let them fall.

Chapter Nineteen

The next day, Kate stayed home, to both his trepidation and his relief. Mikhail called her in the morning, and she actually answered this time.

"I'm much better," she insisted, though she was still a bit hoarse. "I'll be back to work tomorrow."

"Don't rush yourself, Katya."

She laughed. "I'm honestly fine. No fever today. No body aches. My appetite's back."

"Good. Drink more tea. Use another mustard compress. I left the box on your counter by the tea."

"Yes, I will definitely do all of those things."

Her blatant lie made him smile, even while the anxious need to make sure she was healthy and safe was still nagging at him. "I'll come over. You don't know how to make the tea."

"You can't." Kate's voice lowered. "My roommate's home today."

"Ah." He still wanted to check on her. "Would she recognize me?"

"When she hears your accent, she might put two and two together."

In his best attempt at the classic Chicago cadence, he said, "I don't have an accent."

"You sound like a really bad KGB agent."

Mikhail barked out a surprised laugh.

"How do you do, fellow American?" she went on, imitating him. "I enjoy watching baseball and eating hamburgers. Tell me, what government secrets do you know?"

"You sound like the Count from Sesame Street."

It was Kate's turn to laugh. The light, bubbling sound slipped inside Mikhail's chest and lodged there.

"Let me come over, knyazhna. If your roommate knows who I am, you can tell her I am just very devoted to my employees' wellbeing."

"Devoted, huh?" she asked, amused.

"Yes," he said sincerely. "Completely."

There was a pause on her end. After a moment, she said, "Alright. Naomi's out running errands. You can come over for an hour."

KATE RUSHED FRANTICALLY THROUGH GETTING HERSELF cleaned up. She changed into clean leggings and a comfy, oversized sweater. She brushed her neglected hair and quickly french-braided it back from her face. She went through her morning skin-care routine, but before she could put on even a speck of make-up, the intercom buzzed. Swearing, Kate abandoned her efforts and went to let Mikhail in.

He had clearly come straight from work. He showed up less than twenty minutes after their call ended, dressed in his usual impeccable suit. As soon as Kate opened the door for him, he laid the back of his hand against her forehead, her cheek, the side of her neck. She shivered at the gentle touch, pulling back before she did something embarrassing, like try to kiss him again.

"You look much better today," Mikhail said, open relief in his voice. "But you should have more tea." He bypassed her, going to her kitchen and digging around in the cabinets like he had been there a million times.

Amused, Kate wandered in after him, leaning against the doorway as she watched him assemble ingredients and put the pan on to boil. He glanced over his shoulder at her.

"Katya," he said disapprovingly. "You should sit."

She pulled out a stool from beneath the small island and slid onto it. "Happy?"

"I will be when you are fully healthy again."

"Because then I can fuck you?" She asked in a teasing tone, but the question was real enough. The *feelings* were out of her control now, and she could almost believe that the same thing was happening to Mikhail.

He glanced at her again, heat in his eyes. "Not just that, and you know it."

"Do I?" She hadn't meant to voice that one—it was too vulnerable.

Mikhail paused, setting down the jar of cloves he'd been twisting open. He turned to face her. "You should. I've been —" He cut himself off abruptly, lips still parted on unspoken words as his gaze tracked over Kate's face. His expression was unreadable, but something dark and potent burned in his eyes. He turned away from her, focusing on the spices he'd been measuring out. "Tea first. Then we will speak."

Kate's heart skipped. Her hands shook, and she buried

them in her lap to hide it. The kitchen was quiet except for the sounds of Mikhail making tea, and Kate's heartbeat pounding in her ears. When he finally placed a steaming mug in front of her, she immediately locked her hands around it, gripping it hard despite the painful heat.

"So, Katya."

She stared at him, speechless, nearly ready to scream from nerves.

"I have been thinking."

She swallowed, her mouth suddenly dry.

"I would like to—" He frowned, gaze dropping to her white-knuckled hands clenched around the mug. "You're not drinking your tea."

She swallowed again, wetting her lips with her tongue. "I will. Keep talking."

He paused, staring for a long time at the tea. Finally, he looked back up at her. "I would like to renegotiate the terms of our agreement."

Her heart skipped again, then resumed beating in a frantic, staccato rhythm. "Oh?"

"I want more than what we have right now."

Kate couldn't speak. Happiness and excitement and a healthy dose of fear all collided chaotically inside her mind, turning her lungs to rocks and her stomach to a riot of butterflies.

"I want you with me always. When I travel, I want you to come with me. When I'm home, I want you home with me." He paused. "At your leisure, of course. I'm not looking for a slave." A rakish smile curled his lips. "That's my role."

"What exactly are you asking for?" Kate asked, helpless to conceal the excitement in her voice, in her eyes. "Spell it out for me."

"I want you to own me full-time, knyazhna. Leave your job—you won't need it when I'm serving you. You'll have a new job title, with a queen's salary, and better benefits than anyone could ask for."

It took Kate a second to realize that he wasn't speaking figuratively. He meant that she would have an actual job and an actual compensation package.

"A job title?" she repeated slowly, a sinking feeling in her stomach.

"Yes. I've had my assistant put a few different options together. You can choose whichever one you like. I'll have her email the proposals to you."

Proposals—as in, *business* proposals. Still just a job. Kate shook her head slowly, not quite able to process what he was saying to her. "I don't understand. Why do I need a job title? That seems more complicated than—" Than what? Just being his *girlfriend*? Just being cared for because he wanted to, and not because he was contractually obligated to?

"Maybe it is," Mikhail acknowledged calmly, oblivious to the pain twisting Kate's heart. "But this is still an arrangement, and a job title reflects that. Plus, it protects you. All the money I give you will be legally accounted for and taxed, so no financial gray areas to contend with. And, when our time together ends, you'll need something to put on your resume so that you don't have a gap in employment."

Kate couldn't think of a single thing to say to that. She was hurt, but she shouldn't be. Their relationship had been a financial transaction from the start. It was silly of her to feel so blindsided by the fact that it would continue to be nothing more than business. It was foolish of her to have thought that when he said he wanted "more" that he wanted a *real* relationship, and not just more of the service she was already providing.

"I..." She blinked, and then blinked again. She was *not* going to cry. "I don't know. I don't think..." Oh, god, she was definitely going to cry. "No," she said abruptly.

Mikhail frowned. "No?"

Kate got up and crossed the kitchen to the sink. She poured the tea out. "You should go. Naomi will be back any minute."

His frown deepened. "Have I insulted you? What I'm offering is much more—"

"No. I'm not insulted. But I'm also not going to leave my current job to be your full-time mistress."

"But you're fine with part-time?" Mikhail asked incredulously.

As well he might. It was a ridiculous line to draw, from a purely pragmatic standpoint. But pragmatism hadn't entered the equation at all. Instead, her leaden stomach and bruised heart had made the call immediately.

"I can't be entirely dependent on your goodwill for my survival," Kate told him—a half-truth that hadn't occurred to her until she'd had to find a way to explain her rejection.

"Women all over the world depend on a man's income— and I have far more income than most. You could do worse than me."

"Are you talking about *marriage?*" Kate stared at him.

"No," he answered quickly, a flash of shock breaking through the usual stoniness of his expression. "Marriage is... I will never marry. But this is *better*, Katya. Safer. Clearer. More reliable."

A pang of sympathy prevented her from answering right away. *Safer. Clearer. More reliable.* He'd rather pay an employee to perform all the duties of a lover, than to take the risk of having a real relationship.

"Not for me," she finally said. "I can't upend my whole life for a crazy job that isn't even going to last."

Mikhail visibly flinched at that, looking stricken.

"You said it yourself," Kate reminded him, feeling a stirring of anger. He wasn't the one who ought to be hurting right now. "You said it was temporary—that I'd need a job title to put on my resume after you cut me loose."

He ran his hand over his head, raking furrows in his short, dark hair. "Katya, I didn't mean—" He cut himself off, staring helplessly at her, brow furrowed as if she were a puzzle to be solved. "What do you want, then?"

She wasn't about to bare her heart just so he could stomp on it. "I want things to stay how they are," she lied. "I keep my day job. We keep... doing what we're doing."

"You don't even know what I'm offering. The salary, the benefits—"

"I don't want it."

"I can give more. Tell me what you want. A house? Several houses?"

"No." Kate swallowed against the knot rising in her throat.

"Katya, *please!*" he burst out, his deep voice raw with frustration. "Tell me what you want!"

"I don't want to commit to something that you're already planning an ending for!" she snapped, goaded into it by his own failing control.

He went still, imploring expression fading into remote inscrutability again. "You are concerned about what comes after this?"

No, you oblivious dick, she wanted to scream at him. *I'm concerned that you make my stomach flutter and my heart skip, meanwhile all I am to you is a temporary toy.*

"I can make it so that you never have to worry about money again, even after our arrangement runs its course. Your benefits package includes Domovoy stock—the dividends would be enough to live very comfortably off of. The severance package would be equally generous."

For the space of a few seconds, the appeal of guaranteed financial security overwhelmed her. But when she tried to imagine spending the rest of her life trapped in unrequited love with the man who'd paid all her bills but didn't give a shit about her, it crushed any practical considerations. "That's not what I want."

"Nothing," he snapped. "You want nothing."

"I want what we've currently got. That's not nothing." At least this way the lines were clear. She still had her own life. And when he walked away from her, as he'd made clear he would eventually do, Kate wouldn't be left in the position where everything she had was dependent on him.

Mikhail stared at her, speechless, cold. The silence stretched on, tense and brittle. Finally, he pushed away from the counter. "I should get back to the office."

Kate nodded, a foreboding feeling running down her spine. "Are you done with me, then?" she asked quietly.

He turned his head sharply, looking at her as if she were insane. "Do you think I made it to where I am because I give up easily, knyazhna?"

The pet name—she'd long-since stopped thinking of it as an honorific—eased the worst of her worry. He wasn't happy, but he wasn't ending things.

At least not yet.

"Then where do we stand?"

"Apparently in the same place as we did yesterday." He adjusted the knot of his tie, ran a hand down the rest, smoothing it. The gesture had the air of a boxer taping his hands. "If you feel well enough tomorrow, will you come to me?"

She nodded. "Okay."

He held her gaze for a moment longer, before finally turning away and heading for the door. At the threshold, he paused. He reached out, almost nervously, and gently touched her cheek. Kate stared up at him, so hungry to lean into his touch, but afraid to.

"I'll convince you," he assured her.

She couldn't help but smile at his arrogance. "You can try."

Rueful, he stepped back, breaking off the gentle touch. "Goodbye, Katya."

"Goodbye, Mishka."

He froze for a second, dark eyes meeting hers. He opened his mouth as if to say something, then quickly thought better of it. With one last look, he departed.

Chapter Twenty

Later that afternoon, Naomi returned to the apartment, loaded down with shopping bags.

"Hey," she said, huffing as she hauled her bags to the kitchen island. "Got something for you."

"For me?" Kate followed her curiously.

Arms freed, Naomi reached into one of the bags and pulled out a rumpled white envelope. "Okay, don't shoot the messenger—this is from your sister."

Kate's lungs seemed to freeze. "I told you not to let her in!"

"I didn't let her in. She was hanging out by the entry. I think she was asking everybody who went in if they knew you."

Kate accepted the envelope, brow furrowed. "Did she seem... okay?"

"I guess? I don't know what she's normally like, so it's hard to say."

"She didn't insult you or threaten you?"

"No," Naomi said quickly, shocked. "Would she?"

"I don't know. Probably not." Kate reluctantly opened the envelope. She wasn't sure what to expect, but she definitely hadn't been expecting to find a stack of twenties. "What the hell?" she muttered, counting them out. Two hundred dollars, with a small note that read, *For the damages.* Her broke, homeless, addict sister had sent her *two hundred dollars?* Guilt like she hadn't felt in years soured her stomach and gave her an instant headache.

"Are you okay?" Naomi asked gently.

"I'm fine. I... I have to call my mom."

Kate went to her bedroom and shut the door. The phone rang for so long, Kate was sure it was going to voicemail, but at the last second, her mom answered.

"Hello?"

"Hey, mom. Have you heard from Angel lately?"

"Oh, I'm doing alright. Thanks for asking," her mom said airily.

Kate ground her teeth together, but when she spoke, she made sure her voice was patient and unruffled. If she got snappy, Mom would get snappy right back, and then she'd never get the information she needed. "Glad to hear it, Mom. Have you heard from Angel?"

"Not for a couple weeks. Why?"

"Do you know where she is?"

"She's in Chicago. You knew that. Why are you asking? Is she in trouble?"

"Is she still in Chicago?"

"Last I heard. Got a spot at a real high-end club, she says."

Kate doubted very much that Angel's bony ass got a place at a "high end" club, but the news that she was making money was good. "Do you know the name of it?"

"Uh..." Her mom thought for a second. "The Cathouse, I think."

"The Cathouse?" Kate repeated, making sure she heard correctly.

"Maybe," her mom replied uncertainly. "It was something to do with cats."

"Alright. I've got to let you go, okay?"

After bidding her mom goodbye, Kate looked up Chicago strip clubs. There was no Cathouse, but she did find one called *The Cat's Meow*. She called them.

"Cat's Meow," a bored-sounding woman answered. "Open four p.m. to four a.m. Wednesday through Sunday. Fifteen dollars at the door. How can I help you?"

"Hey, I know the answer is already no, but I'm trying to find my sister. If I tell you her name, can you just confirm if she's *not* working there?"

The woman sighed. "Do you know how many bullshit stories I hear from people trying to track down our dancers?"

"I can't even begin to guess at the number, but I know it's bad. My sister's been working at strip clubs for ten years, I've heard the horror stories. Her real name is Angela Pasternak. Can you just confirm that you *don't* have a dancer by that name?"

"I can't give out our dancers' information."

"Right, but I'm asking you to tell me that she's *not* one of your dancers."

"*Girl*," the woman said impatiently. "Listen to me: I cannot give out information on *any* of our dancers. Get it?" She spoke slowly, emphatically.

"I know, but—"

"Think about it. If a girl is working here, I can't say anything about her. Understand?"

Comprehension dawned suddenly. "*Oh*, right. Right. Got it. Well, thanks for your time."

"Sure."

An hour later, Kate was in Pilsen, standing outside an old brick building that had probably been a shoe factory or something like that in the eighteen-hundreds. The heavy steel entry door was painted hot pink, with a stenciled black paw print in the middle. A bright pink and purple neon sign hung over the door, spelling out *The Cat's Meow*.

A burly, bearded, bald-headed white dude with a walkie-talkie clipped to his heavy black Carhartt jacket stood at the door. Kate walked up to him, oddly comforted by his stern, hard-eyed stare. The last time Kate had had to show up at one of Angel's clubs, the bouncer had been obviously strung out and had tried to hit on her. This guy looked more likely to scold her for even being here.

"Hey, can you—"

"ID," he interrupted her.

"I'm not trying to get in. My sister works here, and I have something for her. Can you give this to Angel Pasternak?" Kate held out the envelope.

The bouncer eyed it skeptically.

"It's just cash. Look." Kate opened the envelope, showing him the twenties.

"I'm not going to be the middleman for whatever you're trying to buy."

"I'm not buying anything," Kate said impatiently. "I'm trying to give *my sister* her money back."

"Look, honey, I'm not touching—"

"What the fuck are *you* doing here?" a familiar voice called across the parking lot.

Kate and the bouncer both turned to see Angel walking up to them, a duffel bag slung over her shoulder. If it weren't for her voice, Kate wouldn't have recognized her right away. Her roots had been covered, her hair dyed raven black now. Her nails had been filled too. Her face was all made up, with dramatic eyeshadow and better lashes. She was still too thin, still had the wonky face tattoo, and as she closed in, Kate could see she still had little sores dotting her face—though they were well-concealed by her makeup.

"Angel," Kate said uncomfortably. "Hey."

Angel snorted a skeptical laugh. "Looking for work?"

"I came to give you this." Kate held out the envelope.

Angel didn't even look at it. "How'd you know I was here?"

"Mom told me."

"That loudmouth bitch."

"Can you just take this?" Kate asked, flapping the envelope at her.

Angel finally looked at it. She crossed her arms. "No."

"Please take it. I don't need it."

"Too bad. It's yours now."

Kate tried to tuck it into her sister's crossed arms, but Angel jumped back. "Fuck off!"

"Just take this back!" Kate shoved it at her.

Angel caught her wrist, holding her at arm's length. "No! It's yours!"

"I don't want it!" Kate transferred it to her free hand and tried shoving it into the side pocket on Angel's duffel bag.

Angel twisted, then caught Kate in an unexpected headlock.

"Let go of me you fucking psycho!"

Angel laughed, ruffling Kate's hair. "Nope. Not until you say you'll keep the money."

Kate managed to catch the bouncer's eye. He'd watched their entire scuffle without so much as batting an eyelash. "Aren't you going to do something?" she demanded.

He raised his eyebrows. "I look out for the dancers, not random girls who start shit."

"I was trying to give her her money back!"

The bouncer shifted his focus to Angel. "Is this how you want to be?"

After a pause, Angel sighed, releasing Kate.

Kate straightened her hair and clothes in a huff. "Take the money," she said flatly, dropping it on top of Angel's duffel bag and turning to leave.

Angel snatched it up and thrust it back at her. "If you don't take it, I'll spend it on pills. You really want to knock me off the wagon?"

Kate turned back. "You're sober?"

Angel shrugged.

"Yes or no. Are you clean?"

Angel rolled her eyes. "Yeah. For two weeks now."

Kate was happy to hear it, but knew better than to get her hopes up. Angel had gotten sober for a few weeks at a time over and over again, only to lapse back into using again every time.

"Well. Good. I'm happy for you. But I'm still not taking that cash. Seriously, I'm not trying to be a cunt, but you need it more than I do. It didn't cost me anything to get the wall patched—building maintenance handled it."

"What about the shit I wrecked?"

"That lamp was like ten dollars from Big Lots. And the picture frames were even less than that."

Angel slipped a twenty from the envelope and handed it over.

"Angel—"

"My sobriety is feeling very fragile right now."

"You're such a bitch." Kate pocketed the bill.

The sight of a real smile from Angel suddenly made Kate's throat tighten. She couldn't remember the last time she'd seen one.

"Well, uh, I've got to get back to work," Kate lied.

"Okay." Angel's smile faded, and she was back to looking like a gaunt stranger. "See you."

"Yep. Ah... have a good night."

"Sure."

On the train ride back home, Kate couldn't help but think guiltily about how much Anna had done to save her addict brother, while Kate had more or less cut all ties with her addict sister. As the city raced by the windows, she tried to rationalize the difference. For one, Anna was just a better person than Kate was. She didn't doubt that. But more crucially, money mattered. Anna had been able to get a lawyer to represent Theo for the drug charges—getting felony charges knocked down to misdemeanors—and she'd also been able to pay for in-patient rehab.

Kate could never have done any of those things for Angel. Plus, Theo had actually complied with Anna's wishes, whereas Angel would probably chew off her own foot to escape if Kate ever tried putting her in rehab.

But why were Anna and Theo so different from Kate and Angel?

The answer was still money. Anna and Theo had grown

up middle class. They'd never had to decide whether to eat expired food or go hungry. They'd never had to use dish soap as shampoo. They'd never had to go to school commando because neither of their parents had bought them new underwear in over a year. Angel and Kate had grown up living every moment in survival mode. Kate had survived by detaching from her family so that they didn't drag her down with them. Angel had survived by clinging to whatever scraps of pleasure she could find, never mind that they were self-destructive.

But Kate had money in the form of a pet billionaire. She just had to play her part, and she could make the changes she'd needed when she was a kid.

She pulled her phone out and texted Anna.

Give me the names of some good charities that help children in poverty.

Chapter Twenty-One

Kate arrived at Mikhail's the next night on a tide of mixed feelings. The raw hurt of realizing her deepening feelings were entirely one-sided stood in direct opposition to her libido, which was eager to play after several days of necessary respite.

David showed her up to Mikhail's study right away and then left for the evening, as he—and the rest of the household staff—did every time Kate was over. Would that change if Kate accepted Mikhail's proposition? If she was with him every day, all day, the staff couldn't be expected to vacate the premises every time she and Mikhail wanted to fuck.

It was pointless to wonder. She couldn't accept his offer, and so the question was moot. She forced herself instead to focus on what she *could* have, which was this particular moment, where Mikhail was entirely hers, and questions of love didn't matter. His devotion, in this regard, was unshakeable.

"Hello, knyazhna," he greeted her from his seat behind

his desk, folding his laptop closed as she stepped into the room.

Instead of a greeting, she walked up to his desk and laid a slip of paper down in front of him. Written on it was the name of a non-profit that provided clothing to children in need, especially outerwear like boots and jackets.

"I want a hundred thousand sent here."

Mikhail frowned down at the paper, then up at Kate. "I'll happily give money to *you*, knyazhna. Why won't you—"

"Did I ask for your input? Or did I give you an order?"

"Knyazhna," he began in a conciliatory tone. "Let me—"

"Do I need to remind you of your place? Keep arguing, and you'll see what it gets you."

Mikhail paused for a moment, his gaze tracking over her face. She could see the indecision warring behind those glittering, dark eyes. He wanted to obey. He wanted to be punished. She marked the exact moment when the masochist defeated the obedient slave. His expression didn't shift dramatically, but took on an arrogant slant. He leaned back in his chair, a lazy, insolent posture.

"I'm not trying to argue with you, knyazhna," he lied, a hint of a smile pulling at the corners of his mouth. "I just want to serve you in the best way that I can. And I think the best way—"

"You *think?*" Kate echoed sharply. She circled around the desk, coming up behind Mikhail's chair. He tried to spin to face her, but she caught the back of the chair, keeping him in place. "Who asked you to *think?*"

She slid her hands to his shoulders, leaned down, and smoothed her palms over his broad chest. She felt the shallow rise and fall of his breath. She curled her fingers, dragging her fingernails over the thin, fine weave of his shirt, back up his chest.

"I—"

She clasped one hand around his throat, not tight, just a threat. "Shh. You could have been a good, obedient boy, and I would've rewarded you. But you chose to be mouthy and belligerent, and now here we are. I'll give you one more chance." She tightened her grip, squeezing the sides of his neck. "Send the money, and we can forget all this. I might even let you come."

A shudder ran through him, like a stallion twitching flies off his hide. "But, knyazhna, wouldn't you rather—"

She tightened her grip again, pressing in deeply to the thudding pulse on either side of his muscular neck. "I would rather my slave did as he was told, but it looks like I'll have to beat obedience into him."

Hot, dizzying pleasure sang through Mikhail's veins, spangled over his skin. He desperately wanted to yield to Kate's commands, to please her, but the potency of her ire was too good to pass up. He was lightheaded with it—though that might've been her fingers squeezing his carotid arteries.

As if she could read his mind, she suddenly released her hold on him. "Get up," she ordered icily.

He turned the chair around and stood unsteadily to face her.

"Take your suit off. I never gave you the right to wear clothes around me."

He undressed with deliberate slowness, watching with pleasure as those flame-blue eyes snapped and sparked with irritation at his pace. She couldn't accuse him of disobedience.

But she didn't need to. When his suit coat was on the floor, and his shirt halfway unbuttoned, she reached out and tore the rest of his shirt open. Buttons popped off, pinging against the desk and bouncing on the floor. His dick was instantly hard.

"Knyazhna—"

"I never gave you permission to speak to me." Her hands went to his belt, undoing it roughly, and whipping it out of his belt loops. She doubled it over and slapped it against the palm of one hand, a clear threat. "Move a little faster, or I'll find a way to motivate you."

For a moment he was frozen, torn between the mindless pleasure of obedience and the dark thrill of punishment.

"Well, alright," Kate said, cruel amusement in her voice. "We can do it the hard way."

The decision was made for him, and he melted into it with ease. Even so, he couldn't help but provoke her. If he was going to be punished, he didn't want her holding back. "Please, knyazhna, don't—"

"What did I say about talking?"

He fell silent, his whole body alight with desire and anticipation, a fine tremor going through his hands.

She lifted her chin, a cruel smile turning her sharp-eyed, golden beauty into something almost painful to behold. "Bend over your desk."

He turned, pressing his palms to the smooth, cool surface. He'd sat at this very desk and brokered deals with the richest men in the world. He'd been consulted by heads of state at this desk. He'd upended entire industries with decisions he'd made here. And he was about to desecrate all that power in service to the most singular woman he'd ever known. She boiled his blood and set his soul on fire. He didn't really believe in souls, but Kate had taken hold of something inside him that he'd never felt before, something he had no name for. She owned him more deeply than he'd known he could be.

"Lower." Her silky command brushed his ear, a whisper of breath, the faintest brush of her lips.

He obeyed, bringing himself down to brace his weight on his forearms.

She laughed, a dangerous sound. "*Lower.*"

He sank down even further, bringing his bare chest to the cool surface of his desk, folding his arms in front of his face. The silver medallion clinked against lacquered wood, a sound as final as a bullet being chambered.

One of Kate's hands descended gently onto the small of his back, pressing down as if to pin him in place. The sound of his belt, leather sliding against leather, came from behind him as she shifted her hold on it.

"One stroke for each time you questioned me. Do you know how many that was?"

"No, knyazhna, I wasn't—"

"And we add one more to the tally," she said with cool amusement. "That's a total of eight. You will apologize to me after each one. Understand?"

"Yes, knyazhna." His dick was a rampant pike, so sensitive, he was certain he could feel each individual air molecule vibrating against it.

The first blow landed immediately across his ass. He heard the sound first—a crisp, sharp crack. A split-second later, the pain hit him, white-hot and somehow clarifying, bringing his awareness of his whole body into stark focus. He grunted, hands clenching on nothing.

"What do you have to say for yourself?" Kate prompted.

"I'm sorry, knyazhna!" he gasped, still reeling from the purifying wash of pain.

"For what?"

"For my disobedience."

"I'm glad to hear it. Unfortunately, you've got seven more strokes to go. Ready?"

Before he could answer, the next one landed, just above the last one. That bright white pain cleaved through him again, and he welcomed it with a shuddering groan.

"What do you say?" Kate asked.

"I'm sorry, knyazhna!"

"Don't make me remind you again. Every forgotten apology is another stroke of the belt. Got it?"

"Yes, kny—*ah!*" The third blow landed on the backs of his thighs, making him jump with shock as fresh pain bloomed beneath his skin and electrified his senses.

"I'm sorry, knyazhna!" he cried hoarsely, face buried against his arms.

The fourth strike hit him on the ass again, right across the stinging flesh that the first strike had raised. The layered pain brought a whole new level of shock to his senses, tearing an agonized cry from his throat.

"I'm sorry, knyazhna!"

Again and again, she whipped his belt against his ass and thighs, striping him with pain—pain made ecstatic because it was delivered by her hand. His legs trembled, knees wanting to buckle, as each subsequent blow seemed to intensify, robbing him of strength and balance. But he never forgot to apologize to her. And when the eighth blow landed, he remembered to gasp a ragged, raw-throated apology even as his whole body shook with adrenaline and overstimulation, muscles exhausted from tensing.

"All done," Kate said. Her voice was soft, but there was no gentleness in it.

Mikhail let himself sink to his knees, and when that wasn't enough, he slid off the desk entirely, sprawling on his back on the floor. Kate stood over him, belt still in hand, looking down with cold disdain. She'd kicked her shoes off at some point—probably for better balance while she belted him—and stood in just sheer, black nylon stockings. She shifted her weight, lifting one stockinged foot to press it to his cheek, grinding his face against the floor. He was achingly hard and leaking pre-come like a faucet.

"Are you ready to be obedient?"

"Yes," he panted, his voice slurred by the pressure of her foot on his face.

"Yes, what?"

"Yes, knyazhna."

She laughed, a soft, dark sound. "Good boy." She pulled her foot off, and stepped back, freeing him. He remained sprawled, pulling in rapid breaths, trying to think around the aching pressure of his dripping cock.

"Arrange the donation, and then I'll let you make up for your bad behavior."

"Yes, knyazhna." He pushed himself up slowly on weak arms. His head spun as he looked around the room. "My phone... I can't..." Gripping the edge of the desk, he dragged himself up to standing. "My phone's in my room. I have to get it."

"Get it, then. I'll follow."

"Yes, knyazhna." Feeling a bit like a wounded bison

being trailed by a hungry lioness, Mikhail walked naked and hurting through the halls to his bedroom on the other side of the house.

KATE FOLLOWED MIKHAIL INTO HIS BEDROOM. FOR A moment, she paused, taken aback by the unexpected intimacy of seeing his bed, and standing in the room where he slept. They'd only ever fucked in his office. This felt different. Intimate. Kate had half a mind to leave, but Mikhail had found his phone on the bedside table and brought it to his ear.

"Sarah," he greeted his assistant. "I need you to arrange a donation to, uh—" He glanced at Kate. She handed over the slip of paper she'd pocketed earlier with the non-profit's details written down. Mikhail accepted it, and read it out to Sarah.

While he spoke to his assistant, his hungry gaze pinned on Kate the whole time, she took a moment to look around his room. Large French windows spanned a curved alcove above a cushioned window seat. They were leaded in a diamond pattern and overlooked the backyard with the fountain and the elaborate, but dormant, garden. His bed was a large, wooden four-poster, with dark green bedding. The same Old World architectural details that filled the rest of the house could be found here—high ceilings, wide crown molding, a beautifully parqueted floor.

There wasn't much in the way of personal effects—no photographs, no mementos, no knick-knacks. There was art on the walls, but just like the parlor, it was mostly stuff that seemed to have been curated for the Rich Person Lives Here aesthetic, rather than for any kind of personal touch that seemed unique to Mikhail.

"Yes. Thank you, Sarah." He ended the call and tossed the phone aside. It landed with a noisy clatter on top of a nightstand. "Satisfied?" he demanded.

Kate drew up close to him, pressing herself against him as she ran her hand down his chest, down his stomach. His sullen gaze softened, heated, as her touch drifted lower. She traced her fingers lightly from his hip bone to the crease where his thigh met his groin. With a deft movement, she took hold of his balls.

He stiffened, but didn't dare pull away. "Knyazhna," he breathed. Despite the threat of her grasp, he was hardening again, his cock jutting against her abdomen.

"You never thanked me," Kate told him in a dangerously soft voice.

"Thanked you for what?"

She tightened her grip on his sac, tugging a little. He groaned, leaning into the pull.

"You never thanked me for the privilege of being used for my wishes."

"Ah." He let out a shuddering breath. "Thank you, knyazhna."

She tugged a little harder, making him grunt. His cocked pulsed eagerly. "That didn't sound very sincere."

"Thank you, knyazhna," he growled, eyes squeezed shut as he drew in bracing breaths. "Thank you for using me."

She gave his sac one more tug before releasing him. "That's better. Get on the bed. On your back."

He obeyed, sprawling across the mattress, turning his head to watch her approach. She clambered over him, hiking her skirt up to slide astride his thighs. His cock lay hard and hot and thick against his belly, twitching with each beat of his pulse. She ran a single fingertip along the shaft, a featherlight touch that made him groan with frustration, hips rocking to seek more sensation.

"I'm not done using you," Kate told him, teasing her finger over the sensitive crown of his cock, smiling when she drew another tortured groan from him. "That's what you're for, isn't it?"

"Yes," he breathed eagerly, hips rocking again. "Yes, knyazhna. Use me."

She gripped his shaft and rose up on her knees, pulling her panties aside and guiding his cock to fit the head against her slick folds. His hands went to her hips, gripping her as she sank down on him. They both moaned as she took him into her body, feeling the slow stretch of her inner muscles around his thick, hard shaft. She sank all the way down and rested there for a moment, letting her body acclimate to him.

Mikhail was breathing like a racehorse, his fingers curled into her hips hard enough that she'd probably have marks tomorrow. She didn't mind. She loved how thoroughly she destroyed his self-control.

She rocked slightly, forward and back, feeling him move inside her.

"Ah, fuck, knyazhna, you feel so good."

"You feel good, too," she said, a little breathless as she began to ride him. Up and down at first, mostly just to torment him.

"Fuck, no, knyazhna, please—I'm going to—*agh*—going to come!"

"You better not."

He squeezed his eyes shut, teeth gritted against the pleasure of her body.

She laughed. "Look at you. My perfect sex toy. Always hard when I want a ride."

"Please, please, I need to come. I need to. Knyazhna—" He growled with frustration as she lifted off of him entirely. "No, knyazhna, please, I'm sorry. Take me inside you. I'll be good. Please, knyazhna. *Please*. I need—"

She worked her panties down her legs and over her feet. Balling them up, she stuffed them in his open mouth, cutting him off mid-word.

"Sex toys don't talk," she said.

And then she had him in hand again, guiding him back inside her. She rode him the way *she* liked now, a back and forth grind that worked his pubic bone against her clit while rocking his shaft against a sensitive spot inside her. He writhed beneath her, wordless moans coming from his gagged mouth. It was all so perfect, and with a few more hard grinding rolls of her hips, Kate tipped herself over into a breath-stealing, leg-trembling, toe-curling orgasm.

Mikhail shouted something incomprehensible as her pussy clenched down on him, over and over, and over. When the last ecstatic contraction eased, she drew back until his cock slipped out of her and she sat on his thighs, catching her breath. Mikhail was still throbbing and hard, moaning desperately through her panties.

Prickly with sweat, she reached behind herself to unzip her dress and pull it up over her head. She tossed it to the floor and then sent her bra along with it. Mikhail lifted his head, took in the sight of her naked body, then let his head drop back, uttering a string of Russian curses muffled by her panties.

Still a little breathless, Kate smiled wickedly and took him in hand, stroking up and down.

"You better not come," she warned as she gripped him tighter and pumped faster. "You don't have permission yet."

His inarticulate objections only made her laugh. She kept working his cock, until he was nearly sobbing with the effort of not coming, balls drawn tight, spine bowed, thighs clenched, hands fisted in the bedding.

"No, no, no, no," he begged through the gag. "Nyet. Please, knyazhna. *Ah!* Pozhaluysta!"

When his muffled pleading had shifted to mostly Russian, and he was just about to lose control, Kate let go of his cock. He let out a long, desperate, soul-deep groan, hands clenching and unclenching, hips rocking compulsively. The normally stoic, hard-faced man was flushed and glassy-eyed, totally sex drunk and utterly at Kate's mercy.

She watched him, momentarily stunned by the strength and power of his big body—and that all that strength was hers to command. She felt special, elevated, but also slightly humbled that he trusted her this much. The affection, the closeness, that she'd been trying to fight suddenly overwhelmed her, and she wanted nothing more than to make him feel as good as possible.

She fitted herself against his cock again, sinking down, taking him in. She sat there, holding him inside, stroking her hands soothingly over his chest. Bracing her weight on her hands, she started to work her hips.

"You want to come?"

He moaned. His whole body shook.

"Do what you want," she told him. She reached up to pluck her panties out of his mouth. "Come for me, Mishka."

His hands went to her hips again, gripping tight, and he flipped her onto her back. He was on top, all that weight bearing down between her thighs, but there was still no mistaking who was in control. Kate clung to him like a rider on a particularly rowdy stallion, while Mikhail labored at her command, breathing hard, dazed eyes searching hers with a softness that only existed in moments like these.

Kate cupped the back of his neck, urging him on, rolling her hips to meet his desperate thrusts. "Come for me," she panted. "Be a good boy and—"

His mouth descended on hers, stealing her words. Stunned, Kate held onto him and kissed him back with the same wild abandon as they fucked. It meant something, she knew, that he'd initiated the kiss. That he needed it so desperately, so urgently. She bit his bottom lip and sucked on his tongue, making him growl and buck into her harder.

And then he was coming, and the feel of him shaking and shuddering on top of her, the hot, wet spill of his climax, the agonized groan rumbling deep in his throat, all conspired to force another orgasm out of Kate. Mikhail made a pained, almost animalistic noise as her pussy clenched around him again, milking every last drop from him.

When the last wracking spasm released him, Mikhail slumped on top of Kate, driving the breath out of her in a faint, "*Oof.*" His weight wasn't unpleasant. In fact, there was something kind of soothing about being slightly crushed. But Mikhail wasn't moving at all, and it was mildly concerning. Kate twisted to look him in the eye. Mute, dazed, he stared vacantly through her, pulling in slow, rasping breaths.

Well. At least he was breathing.

Kate touched his cheek. "Honey," she said gently—only becoming aware of the endearment after it had already left her mouth. "Mikhail," she corrected herself, but that sounded wrong too. "Mishka," she said gently, stroking his cheek.

At that, he blinked, drawing in a deep breath. He closed his eyes, leaning into her touch. She brought her other hand up to cup his face, stroking gently along his neck and shoulders, over his back. He shuddered and sighed, but remained putty beneath her hands.

"Are you alright?" she asked softly.

He let out a wry, wheezing laugh. "No. I think you killed me."

"You're a very talkative corpse."

He chuckled again, his breath gusting against the side of her neck. "Why are you so good, Katya? You're a succubus. You're stealing my soul through my dick."

"You caught me."

"Don't stop. I don't need a soul."

She smiled. "Well, I need to breathe. Get off of me, you oaf."

He groaned like an old dog and rolled off of her. Cold air hit her skin unpleasantly, like being thrown into a pool. She shivered, but not for long. Mikhail's arms snaked around her, pulling her on top of him.

She lay ensconced in his arms, her head resting on his chest, feeling the rise and fall of each breath, listening to the steady beat of his heart. He shifted minutely, and she felt the press of his lips to the top of her head. She breathed out a contented sigh, stroking her fingertips through the dense mat of his chest hair. She brushed against the medallion, tracing its edges.

"Why do you always wear this?" she asked, too pleasure-dazed to filter her thoughts properly.

To her surprise, though, he actually answered her. "It was a gift given to me as a child."

She knew he had no family. Who would have given him

a gift so personal that he still wore it to this day? She hesitated to voice the question, but she didn't need to.

"One of the matrons at the orphanage gave it to me. She recognized my academic potential and fought to have me transferred to a better school. Her support changed the trajectory of my entire life. When I was thirteen, I was sent to an elite boarding school on a scholarship, thanks to her efforts. She died right before I finished my baccalaureate, so she never saw what became of me."

Kate was awed that he'd revealed so much—that he'd trusted her with something of such obvious emotional significance. She stroked the medallion contemplatively. "She'd be proud of you if she could see you."

"I don't think she would," Mikhail said quietly.

"No?"

"She gave me this to remind me to be humble and grateful. She didn't approve of immense wealth. A bit like you, in that regard."

"Why do you wear the medal, then?"

"To remember her." He paused. "To remember who I was."

"Who were you?"

"An unwanted castaway who shouldn't have amounted to anything."

Kate pushed herself up onto one elbow, looking down at him. She stroked her hand across the furry plane of his chest. "You were always going to amount to something."

"Nobody knew or cared who I was until I proved I could make them money. A *lot* of money. Now I make my own money, and the world only loves me more for it."

"Money doesn't make you. Your inventions contributed more to the world than your wealth ever will."

Mikhail gave her a skeptical look.

"Look, I don't know a lot about computer science. But I do know that the processor that you developed when you founded Domovoy has increased tech accessibility all over the world. Hospitals and schools and homes all have better tech than they could have afforded before your invention. It's improving lives all over the world."

"Because it's cheap to produce from materials that are easy to source," Mikhail said dismissively. "It still comes down to money."

As she struggled to find a way to convince him that he was so much more than the wealth he'd accumulated, Kate realized she'd gotten way too deeply invested. The urgency she felt, the desperate need to make him see the things she valued in him, it was too much. She couldn't keep doing this with him and pretending she didn't feel this way.

"Not everybody cares about money," she said.

His gaze cut to her, contemplative, a little bitter, even. "Not you. How much money do I have to throw at you to make you take me up?"

Nothing ventured, nothing gained, right? Kate had to believe that Mikhail's blindness to his own innate worth was the only barrier between what she wanted and what he was offering. He wouldn't want her this badly, treat her this sweetly, if she was just a paid service. Just a transaction.

"I don't want money. I want more than that. I want... I want a real relationship."

Mikhail went utterly still. "What?"

"I don't want to be your employee. I want to be your... girlfriend? Partner? I want something *real*."

He stared at her. "Katya..." He spoke her name with obvious reluctance, looking uneasy.

Well. There was her answer. She pulled away from him immediately, slipping out of bed to find her clothes. Mikhail sat up, watching her, his face a stone mask. "I've never wanted a 'real' relationship," he said apologetically. "I'm not built that way."

"That's fine," Kate said as calmly as she could. "That's your right."

"I don't think I'm even capable of it," he went on. "I never had a family. I've moved around so much, never in one place long enough to build those bonds. After a certain amount of time, that part of the brain just doesn't develop, if it's not stimulated. Like feral children who never learn to speak." He began to sound aggravated, a hint of urgency as he tried to explain.

Kate finished zipping her dress. "It's okay, Mikhail. You don't owe me feelings." She was impressed by how collected she sounded. She managed to speak around the lump in her throat as if it weren't even there.

"I wish I were capable of it, Katya. I know I'd love you, if I could."

A sneaky tear broke the dam, and now her eyes were leaking. She turned her back on him, blinking hard, wiping discreetly at her cheeks. She couldn't even think how to respond to what he'd told her. "Can you tell the driver to come get me? Or I can get an Uber, it's fine. Whatever." The wobble in her voice gave her away, and suddenly Mikhail was out of bed, big hands clasping her shoulders, spinning her around.

"Ah, no, Katya." He stared down at her teary face, deeply aggrieved. "Take the job I'm offering. It's—"

"Nope. No." She shook her head, pulling out of his hold. "Can't do that. And I can't do this—" she gestured between the two of them "—anymore, either. Sorry." She turned away from him again. "Where are my shoes? Did I—oh. I left them in your office. I'm going to go get them, would you call your driver?"

"Katya—"

"If you don't, I'll walk out of here and take the train home."

He sighed. "I wish you would stay, but I won't stop you from leaving."

"Good."

"But we're not done talking about this."

Yes we are. He just didn't know it yet.

Chapter Twenty-Two

Three days had passed since she'd left his house, and Kate wouldn't answer Mikhail's calls or his texts. Knowing it was an asshole move, he did it anyway—on Thursday, he had her called up to his office.

She entered, looking harried and grim. "What is this?" she demanded as soon as the door was closed.

"We need to talk, Katya."

"We did talk. We realized we want different things, so now we're going our separate ways. The end."

Mikhail rose from his desk chair. "*Not* the end. This isn't over. Not yet."

"Not *yet*?" she repeated with a laugh that sounded more pained than amused.

"I've hurt you." He started towards her, but she stopped him with a raised hand.

"I hurt myself by seeing something that wasn't there. That's not your fault."

It was his fault—he was fundamentally broken, and that brokenness had harmed her. And now she was leaving him.

The dull pressure he felt in his chest whenever he was away from her became an unbearable ache. He pressed one fist against it, as if he could crush it into nothing.

"Knyazhna—"

"No. I'm not... that. Not anymore."

"What if I tried?"

She frowned at him. "Tried what? Tried to feel something for me?"

He nodded.

"You can't force what's not there. And I don't want you to pretend. I'd rather have nothing at all than something fake."

"Can't it be enough that I serve you and keep you in luxury?"

"Only until you get bored of me," she said coldly.

It was on the tip of his tongue to tell her that he would never get bored of her. But the words got caught in his throat, and he swallowed them back down.

"Goodbye Mikhail." She turned away from him. At the door, she paused with one hand on the handle. "I turned in my two weeks notice yesterday. You'll forget about me once I'm gone."

The news shattered him. Before she could open the door, he was there, pinning it shut with one hand. "*No.*"

"Yes. Now, let me out." She tugged at the handle.

"What can I do?" he pleaded, feeling as if everything he'd ever earned, everything he'd built, was crumbling beneath him like sand.

She gave him an agonized look, but didn't answer.

"Remember when we talked about Shanghai? I'll take you. Right now."

"That's not what I need. Trips and cars and high-end

jewelry aren't what I *need*. Why can't you understand the difference?"

He couldn't help reaching for her. She was stiff as a statue when he touched her, his hand circling her arm, trying to urge her closer. "What if I married you?" he proposed wildly.

"*Marriage?*" she repeated in a stunned voice.

"Yes. I'll marry you. No prenup. Just don't leave."

She was quiet. Her gaze tracked over his face, brows drawn together. Indecision warred in her eyes, and for a moment, Mikhail dared to hope.

"Does marriage come with love?"

His hope died. He wouldn't lie to her. "I don't know what love is, Katya."

"If you're not capable of love, then I'm not capable of marriage."

"Katya, please. You can't throw away everything I'm offering. It's foolish."

Anger sparked in her eyes. "Maybe I am a fool. I'll probably even regret this, after enough time. Will that make you happy?"

"No!" he burst out wildly. "I will be miserable! Why make us both miserable? Just say yes. Just come back."

"I want to be loved."

"Then I'll tell you I love you! Every fucking day! Will that bring you back?"

"Will you mean it?"

He couldn't answer her.

"Is money the only thing you understand?" she asked tiredly.

"It's the only thing that matters."

"And that's why I can't be with you."

"I misspoke," he said quickly. "You matter, too."

"Would you give up your money to be with me?"

"You know my net worth is all in Domovoy. It would mean giving up control of my company. My life's work."

"You're right. That's asking too much."

Mikhail stared at her. The words sounded right, but he sensed she was slipping even further out of his reach. "I'll give you shares. If you come back to me, I'll give you half my shares."

She frowned. "You wouldn't be majority shareholder, then."

"*We* would be." The idea warmed him.

He could see her indecision—all that wealth would be an intoxicating pull, but was it enough?

"I don't want that responsibility. I don't..." she shook her head, at a loss. "Sitting on a board and voting on corporate decisions had never appealed to me."

"Then what do you want? Tell me, I'll give it to you."

She sighed. "I want you to be somebody you're not. Somebody who has a heart. Somebody I can trust with mine. If you can't be that, then let me go."

He had no choice. He stood back and watched her walk away. A crushing breathlessness stole over him as he returned to his desk. All the money in the world, and he couldn't buy the one thing he wanted most.

Chapter Twenty-Three

After quitting Domovoy, Kate had a lot of free time on her hands. She hadn't yet found a new job, but fortunately, she had nearly forty thousand dollars socked away from Mikhail's weekly payments. She'd be alright for a few weeks, or even months.

So, in between sending out resumes and enduring pointless phone conversations with recruiters offering shit jobs with shit pay, she decided it was time she finally learned to cook. She told herself it was because cooking was a crucial life skill. Deep down, she knew it was because she was desperate for a distraction from Mikhail—it was impossible to deny when she kept using her dented old aluminum stock pot instead of the gorgeous enameled cast iron dutch oven that a certain billionaire had purchased for her.

She couldn't talk to Anna or Naomi about it. She'd signed an NDA. And while she trusted them not to run their mouths, she couldn't bring herself to break the confidence she'd promised to Mikhail. So instead, she threw herself whole-heartedly into trying to recreate her favorite meals from childhood.

But as she stared at the bubbling muck that she'd failed, for the third time, to turn into an edible meal, she had to admit that it wasn't going very well. She'd seen her sister make it a hundred times when they were kids. Spicy chicken casserole. It had looked so easy. Canned chicken, canned cream soup, some veggies, some noodles, and some spices. But every time Kate tried, it was an inedible mess.

She was scraping her third attempt into the trash when her phone lit up. She glanced at it, feeling her heart squeeze at the same time her stomach dropped. She kept hoping it was Mikhail. She also kept dreading it was Mikhail. If he asked her again, she knew she'd give in. She wanted to give in. She also wanted to keep her pride.

She picked up the phone and blew out a breath. Not Mikhail. It was her sister.

"Angel?" she answered hesitantly. "Is everything okay?"

"Yeah. Hey, do you know some, like, Eastern European guy named Michael?"

Kate froze. "Michael? Or Mikhail?"

"Yeah, that's it. Wears an expensive suit. Looks like he doesn't even smile on his birthday."

"Maybe," Kate said uneasily. "How do *you* know him?"

"He came to the club, asked for me specifically, and then all he did was interrogate me about *you* all night long."

"What?"

"Yeah. So, are you in trouble with the Oskolki, or what?"

"The Osko—the what?"

"The Russian mob."

"*No.* Jesus. He's... he's an ex, basically."

"Ahhh." Angel chuckled. "Well, I didn't tell him anything."

Kate rubbed at her forehead.

"He was a *real* good fucking tipper, though. You sure you want to let that one go?"

Kate sighed. "I had no choice."

"Married?"

"No. Just incapable of love, apparently."

"Been there."

A pause followed, and in that pause, Kate realized this was the first time in a long time she'd had a normal conversation with her sister. The urge to keep it going was a new one. Usually she was desperate to escape conversations with Angel.

"So, um, weird question—do you remember that spicy chicken casserole you used to make?"

"Yeah. Why?"

"I've been trying to make it, and it's not turning out at all. Like, it's literally inedible."

Angel clicked her tongue, thinking. "Tell me what you did."

Kate gave her the run-down of every step.

"That's *way* too much cream of chicken soup. You just need one can. And cayenne and paprika aren't interchangeable. If you're using cayenne, then you have to use way less."

"They're both just ground-up peppers," Kate said. She knew that was right—she'd looked it up.

"Yeah, but paprika is ground-up bell peppers which aren't spicy at all. And cayenne is super hot little chilis."

"Oh," she said, feeling stupid.

"And you have to cook down all the veggies until they're

soft before you add any of the other ingredients. Otherwise, they'll be all hard and raw."

"Oh."

"I'll text you the instructions," Angel said with a small laugh.

"Thanks," Kate said. Another lull followed, and she was oddly reluctant to let it stretch out too long. "So, you... you sound like you're doing good."

Angel laughed again, a soft, recriminating sound. "I don't sound hopped up, you mean?"

"Or drunk," Kate admitted.

"Yeah. Still on the wagon. I, uh..." She trailed off, sounding a little embarrassed.

"What?" Kate pressed.

"I met someone, working at Cat's Meow. He's a recovered addict, and he's been, sort of... helping me out."

Kate had never heard Angel sound so bashful. A wicked, sisterly grin stretched her cheeks. "*Helping you out*, huh?"

"Shut up," Angel said, no actual rancor in her voice.

"You liiiike him," Kate crooned.

"Oh my god, shut up, or I'll call your mafia man and tell him everything he wanted to know."

"You *liiike* him and you want to—wait. What did Mikhail want to know? And why do you have his number?"

"He wanted to know what kinds of things you liked. What I thought you wanted most in the world. He left his number, said I should call him if I thought of anything."

He was still trying to buy her. She was so torn. On the one hand, a part of her was thrilled that he was still trying. But another part of her was furious that he still thought he could throw enough money at her and eventually get his way.

"Tell him I want him to make up the budget shortfall for all the public schools in Chicago."

"That's... that's a really specific one there, twinnie."

"And I want him to implement a profit-sharing scheme for all employees at his company, with shareholder voting rights."

"Should I be writing this down?"

"And I want him to start a non-profit dedicated to—"

"Bitch, call him yourself."

Kate laughed and then sighed. "I can't. I'll give in."

Angel made a sympathetic noise. "Don't call him, then. But, between you and me, you're asking for a lot."

"He's, like, *crazy* rich. And he thinks money will make up for not loving me."

"Oh, fuck, suck him dry, then."

Kate laughed.

"Hey, so, I gotta get going. But I'll send you that recipe, okay?"

"Sure, yeah. Thanks. Um, could you send me the tater tot casserole recipe, too?"

"You know you can just find a recipe online."

"Yeah, but I like yours."

There was a faint, shy pause. "Alright. Talk to you later, twinnie."

"Bye."

Kate set her phone back down, feeling strangely light, even with the pain of Mikhail's rejection—whether he saw it that way or not—still consuming her.

———

IF HAVING KATE IN HIS LIFE HAD BEEN A DISTRACTION, not having her was a lobotomy. He wandered through his days in a fog. The mental effort he usually put into his company had been completely diverted to plans for convincing her to come back. He'd tracked down her sister, but it had gotten him nowhere. He'd considered reaching out to her parents, but she'd been clear that her childhood had been terrible. He doubted the people who'd overseen that terrible childhood would have much insight to offer.

Weeks passed, and he drifted through them on autopilot. Domovoy continued to operate, continued to climb in profit and prestige. After a vote, the shareholders approved Domovoy's second stock split. The value of shares shot up almost immediately after, and Mikhail found himself even richer than before, but with none of the comfort those numbers used to provide. Instead, he could only imagine Kate's disdain.

What if he gave her half his shares?

No. She'd already told him no.

What if he appointed her to the board in his place?

Not what she wanted.

She wanted love. The one thing he couldn't buy, couldn't sell, couldn't trade. He rubbed at the hollow spot in his chest. The spot where his heart should be. The spot that should be filled with love for Kate. Instead, it only ached. Sometimes he resented her for the pain. If she'd just be sensible, they could both be happy. Instead, she had to demand the impossible.

After a meeting with the product development team, in which his attention was mostly turned inward on thoughts of Kate, he left the Domovoy building and wandered the city streets like a maudlin cliché. His meandering inadvertently took him to Oak Street. He stood on the corner, watching shoppers mill between high-end storefronts. The last time he'd been here, he'd been buying Kate whatever she wanted. The memory was an uncomfortable one—a happy moment inextricably tied to the distressing memory of her tears. He'd still never figured out why she'd been crying that day. Had she known, even then, that Mikhail couldn't ever give her what she truly needed? Had that day been the beginning of the end?

His phone buzzed in his pocket. He pulled it out, expecting a business call. Instead, it was an unrecognized number with a Wisconsin area code. Instead of dismissing it, something compelled him to answer.

"Hello?"

"Hey, comrade." That raspy voice was familiar, but it took him a second to place it—Kate's sister. He'd spoken to her a few nights ago.

"Ms. Pasternak," he greeted her, his heart suddenly thundering. "How can I help you?"

"I think you know *I'm* about to help *you*."

He paused, not daring to hope. "Are you?"

"Maybe. It depends on you, I guess." The rumble of a man's voice sounded in the background, and she hushed him impatiently. "Anyways, I've been thinking about the things you asked me, and the things my sister told me..." she trailed off teasingly.

"And?" Mikhail prompted impatiently.

"And I think you're both dumber than a bag of hammers."

"Alright. Yes. Thank you. This has been immensely help-ful." Mikhail pulled the phone away from his face, prepared to end the call, but Angel Pasternak's shouted words couldn't be ignored.

"You love her!"

He sighed. "What did she tell you?"

"That you've got a calculator where your heart should be. But, dude, you're acting exactly like a man who's sick in love."

"I don't even know what that means."

"I don't know how magnets work. Doesn't mean they're not real."

That was, oddly, a decent point. Uncertain why he was confessing all this, but aware that he had nothing to lose at this point, he told her, "If I could love anyone, I would love your sister."

"Man, you already do."

"I don't think so. I've never done it before. If I loved her, I'd... I'd do love things."

"What the fuck are 'love things'?"

"I don't know! That's the problem!" He realized belatedly that he was shouting on a street corner like a madman. Turning, he walked away from the hustle of the busy shopping district, back towards Domovoy's offices.

"Okay, so. You want her with you all the time?"

"Yes," he gritted out, deeply uncomfortable.

"And you want to take care of her, make sure she's safe and happy?"

"Yes."

"Wow, don't sound too excited about it." Angel chuckled. "Anyways, that's love. That's literally all love is."

It couldn't be. Love was supposed to be grand and poetic and magical, and all Mikhail felt was a base need—something like hunger or thirst. It was primal and simplistic and far too straightforward to be *love*.

"Look," Angel went on while he stood in stunned silence.

"I don't know what your damage is, but I assure you, love is not as complicated as you're making it. I should know—I've fucked up more good things than most people ever get a chance at. But if you can't recognize that you're in love, and admit it to Kate, you are *never* going to get her back."

Mikhail's chest squeezed like a vise had been clamped around it. *This* was love? This horrible feeling?

"If I tell her—" he began hoarsely, desperately.

"That's not going to cut it," Angel said, a hint of dislike coming through. "You already told her you don't love her. You can't fix that damage with more talk. She'll think you're lying."

"Then what do I do?" He asked, almost relieved. He understood action better than words, anyway.

"That's between you and my sister. But whatever you do, it's got to be enough to override the bullshit you already told her. Prove she's the most important thing to you."

Was she the most important thing? He used to think it was his company, his wealth. He'd as much as told her so. But without her, none of that gave him any of the pleasure that it used to. But what would sacrificing his company accomplish?

"I can hear the gears turning in your skull, so good luck, buddy. I gotta go."

"Yes, well... thank you," Mikhail said.

"Wasn't for you. But I hope you figure your shit out anyway." She hung up.

Mikhail pocketed his phone, walking back to Domovoy slowly, replaying every conversation he'd ever had with Kate about her place in his life. Bit by bit, a pattern emerged. Bit by bit, a plan came together.

Chapter Twenty-Four

"Sounds like you quit your job a few weeks too early," Theo told Kate while Anna dealt cards around the table. They were playing sheepshead because Theo and Kate had managed to ruin cooperative games with their back-and-forth enmity.

"Why do you say that?" Kate asked, pretending disinterest. Any mention of Domovoy had her full attention, mainly because she was hoping for any scrap of news about Mikhail. For the sake of her own sanity, she'd had to use the parental controls on her phone settings to block internet access to anything related to Domovoy or its CEO.

"You didn't hear? They just instituted a huge stock-sharing program with all the employees. It was all over the news today."

"What?"

"Yeah. The CEO—Volkov?—gave up, like, half his ownership shares to start the program. He basically cut his net worth in half overnight."

"He's still got billions," Anna said dismissively.

"I heard the other shareholders are suing to have him kicked off the board and removed from the CEO position," Zach said distractedly, his attention focused on arranging his cards.

"Can they do that?" Mel asked.

Theo shrugged.

"Give me a second." Kate laid her cards down to pull out her phone. She quickly removed the blocked searches from her settings and went to look up the news. Multiple headlines came up, so she clicked on the first link.

In a surprise move, Domovoy Technologies founder Mikhail Volkov has distributed half of his Domovoy shares amongst employees, including the associated shareholder voting rights. Given the size of the company, and the number of employees, Domovoy's employees have opted to vote as a single bloc, electing representatives to attend shareholder meetings. This distribution of shares has reduced Volkov's net worth —previously estimated at 52 billion USD—to less than 30 billion USD.

The move was unilaterally opposed by all other shareholders, but until distributing shares to employees, Volkov held a controlling interest in the company, and his decision could not be overruled by other shareholders. Beginning in the third fiscal quarter, employee shareholders as a collective will have equal share ownership to the CEO and founder.

This move comes just days after it was revealed that Domovoy stock had split for the second time, and share value increased by 30%. When reached for comment, Domovoy's spokesperson released the following brief statement:

"People matter more than money. Especially the people we love."

Volkov, who has previously been a relatively apolitical figure in the financial world, seems to be decisively abandoning that policy.

"Oh." Kate couldn't quite breathe. "So, he's not the majority shareholder anymore? He gave that up for m—for his employees?"

"I guess."

"He might actually be a decent human being," Anna said as she finished dealing. "He's the one who saved Margaret's Arms from closing down."

"Did you know about all this?" Kate asked Naomi.

On the other side of the table, Naomi grimaced. "Yeah, sorry. I didn't bring it up, because you were so upset after quitting. I didn't want to rub salt in the wound." She shot an accusatory glance at Theo.

"No, it's fine. I... I'm fine."

"Maybe they'll hire you back," Naomi suggested. "They kept calling and calling after you quit."

"...Maybe," Kate agreed softly, mind spinning.

The conversation shifted as the game began, and Kate played the worst five rounds of her life. She lost resoundingly each time, earning heckles from Theo and unnervingly contemplative looks from Anna. And for once, she didn't care.

When she and Naomi got home that night, there was a small package sitting in front of their door. It hadn't gone through the mail—it was a plain box, with only Kate's name written on it in blocky letters. She picked it up and carried it inside and then sat on the couch and stared at it.

"Aren't you going to open it?" Naomi asked.

"I'm afraid to."

Naomi backed away a step. "Is it dangerous?"

"No. Not like that." Taking a deep breath, Kate forced herself to rip the tape off.

Inside the plain cardboard box, a square velvet jewelry box was nestled in packing foam. She pulled it out and cradled it in her palm for a minute. If it was an engagement ring, she wasn't sure what she'd do.

"Open it," Naomi urged.

Taking another breath, Kate did. There was no ring inside. Instead, he'd sent her the Marian medallion he'd always worn around his neck.

"Oh my god," she breathed. Her eyes burned and her throat tightened.

"There's a note," Naomi said softly, pulling a slip of paper from the cardboard box. She handed it to Kate.

Knyazhna,
I did not know what love was until you took it from
me. Please give me your heart back, because you
already have mine.
With love always,
Your Mishka.

"Is that the guy who's been texting you?" Naomi asked

excitedly. She gasped. "Is *that* why you quit Domovoy? He was your coworker!"

"Um. Sort of."

At the bottom of the note was a date, time, and a set of coordinates.

"What is this, a scavenger hunt?" Naomi asked, wrinkling her nose.

A scavenger hunt didn't sound very Mikhail-like. Kate picked up her phone to check the coordinates—it brought her to a specific point in Lincoln Park. After a moment, she realized that she knew that particular spot. It was the Chess Pavilion.

He wanted to meet here there. Tomorrow.

Well, that just wasn't going to work.

———

"Mr. Volkov, there's a visitor asking to see you."

Mikhail frowned at Marx. Every once in a while, raving lunatics tried to get into the property, claiming they were invited guests. The staff knew how to handle them.

"Get rid of them," he said impatiently.

"Ordinarily I would, but it's Ms. Pasternak."

Mikhail bashed his knee against his desk as he bolted upright. "Let her the fuck in!" he barked.

"She's already waiting in the parlor."

Mikhail bulldozed past Marx, halfway down the stairs when he called back, "Send all the staff home."

When he reached the parlor, Kate was standing at the window, looking into the yard, her back turned to him.

"Knyazhna," he said hoarsely.

She turned to face him, looking far more grave than he would have hoped for.

"Mikhail," she said softly. Not Mishka.

"Tell me you're here because you're coming back to me," he pleaded, closing the distance between them.

She laid a gentle hand on his chest, halting him before he could wrap his arms around her. She looked up at him, searching his face, seeking something he prayed she would find. "You love me?"

"*Yes*," he said desperately, willing her to believe him. "I didn't know. I didn't know what it was." He grabbed her hand and slid it higher on his chest, right over the part that burned when she was near, and ached hollowly when she was away. "You're in here, knyazhna, burrowed so deep, I didn't realize it until it was too late. Please don't leave me again. Let me prove myself."

He'd begged the same thing of her many times before, but he'd never meant it as much as he did now.

Kate considered him a moment longer, her hand clutched over his beating heart. Finally, with her free hand, she reached beneath the collar of her blouse. She pulled out a tarnished silver chain, and with it, a worn Marian medallion.

"I believe you," she said with a soft smile. "I love you, too."

Mikhail pulled her close, wrapping his arms around her, crushing her body against his. He kissed the top of her head again and again, muttering frantic endearments in two languages. "You'll believe me every day, Katya. Every day. You'll never wonder. I'll do anything you ask. Give you anything you want."

"I want your heart."

"It's yours. It's been yours. I didn't know, but I do now."

"And I want a giant engagement ring."

He straightened, releasing her and reaching for her hand. "We'll go now."

"No, wait," she laughed, tugging against his grasp. "Not yet. My friends have to meet you and get to know you before I can announce an engagement."

"I don't care about them," Mikhail growled.

"But I do."

The rancor faded. "Fine. Then I suppose I care as well."

"Just to warn you, the billionaire thing is not going to endear you to them."

"I gave away half of my ownership!" he objected hotly.

"You're still the CEO. And you're still a billionaire," Kate pointed out.

"They'll have to drag my desiccated corpse out of the CEO's office," Mikhail told her. "And as for the billions... aren't you the woman who claimed she could ruin me?"

Kate gave him that curling, feral little smile he loved so much. "Are you saying I couldn't?"

"There's still plenty of time for you to try." He stepped closer, tilting his chin down as Kate tilted hers up, bringing them face to face. "You don't like billionaires, Katya? Here's your chance to get rid of at least one of us."

"Hmmm... I do like a challenge. And since I'm unemployed right now, it'll give me something to do with my time."

"Ruining me will be a full-time job," he promised. Mikhail had considered, from time to time, establishing a foundation that funded charities and causes that were of interest to him. Promoting STEM education in impoverished communities. Scholarships. Financial aid for immigrant students. But doing such a thing would require him to spell out those interests to another person—to make himself vulnerable in a way that he just wasn't capable of. And so nothing had ever been established.

Until Katya. She knew his every weakness. Knew the shape and depth of his damage, and could be trusted to navigate it. He didn't dare bring up the idea of an actual salaried job just now, but someday soon, when they were on stable footing, and her trust in him was iron-clad, he'd ask her to run the foundation. Her analytical, organized brain would be excellent at it. And she would enjoy trying to bleed him dry.

But for now, he just needed to be with her. To hold her, feel her, care for her. With her face still tilted up to his, he bent down and kissed her. It was soft and sweet and light. He had never kissed anyone this way, never been kissed like this. It stripped him raw, this simple touch, but he savored the burn, because it came from her. Katya. His knyazhna.

Epilogue

"*Agh*, please, knyazhna!"

"Sorry, but you brought this on yourself." She slid her bare foot up his shaft, pressing the sensitive head firmly to his stomach. He lay on his side at her feet, on the floor of his office in the Domovoy building. He was mostly dressed, except for his trousers which had been unzipped and tugged down his thighs, and his necktie, which was currently keeping his wrists tied behind his back.

"I'm going to come," he gritted out as she teased the head of his cock.

"You better not." She slid her foot back down, applying threatening pressure to his balls.

He panted and groaned, writhing restlessly. Her foot pressed down a little harder.

"Hold still."

He froze, except for the tremor that ran through every straining muscle.

"Now, about that ten million—"

"For *politicians!*" he spat out, unable to contain himself.

She pressed harder on his balls, making him grunt, his hips rocking back, away from the punishing pressure.

"For several super-PACs and some worthwhile candidates who are dedicated to overturning Citizens United," she explained patiently.

"I thought you wanted me to be able to use my unfair wealth to influence politics for the better," he said between panting breaths.

"If we can get you and the rest of your ilk out of politics entirely, I'll hardly need your influence."

"'Hardly'?" he echoed, more confident than he had any right to be. "So you'll still need me."

He yelped at the sudden buzz against his prostate. He'd forgotten about the plug.

"Don't get cocky," Kate said. She smiled as he writhed beneath her, begging for mercy.

"Stop, I'm going to come! Please, knyazhna, I can't—*ah*— no, no, no—" The first pulse of climax had him doubling over, groaning. Kate immediately cut the vibrations from the plug and pulled her foot away from his sac, stealing all the sensation so that he felt nothing but pulsing contractions in his core, the wet seep of come spilling from his cock. He swore viciously in English, Russian, and every other language he knew.

The pleasureless, pointless orgasm came to a weak finish, and he sagged against the floor, groaning and gasping for breath.

"Oh no," Kate said with wicked amusement. "Look at the disgusting mess you made. You know what that means. Lick it up."

"Knyazhna, please, no."

"Then release the funds."

He lay there, deliberating. Obedience or punishment? Today, obedience won out. "*Fine,*" he growled. "The money's yours."

She pressed her foot in the puddle of his come, then dragged it across his face, leaving a sticky, smeared streak. "Good boy. Now, go get some toweling and clean this up."

Before he could do that, it took him some time to wriggle his wrists free of the tie, which Kate didn't bother to assist with. Hands freed, he went to get toweling from his bathroom, wetting it at the sink. As he wiped the floor clean, Kate hooked her knees over the arms of his desk chair and stroked her clit. He wasn't allowed to touch or look—continued punishment for his earlier resistance.

"Why aren't you cleaning?" Kate demanded. He'd gone still, listening to her shallow breaths and the soft, slick sounds of her fingers gliding over her wet pussy. "Get to work."

He jarred back into motion, growling when he heard the gasping, whimpering cry stifled behind her own palm that signaled Kate's climax. That he had not been the one to give it to her was the worst possible punishment.

"Knyazhna," he groaned. "This is cruel."

She laughed, slipping one leg off the chair arm to poke his ribs with her toes. "When I see the funds have transferred to the foundation's accounts, I'll let you give me an orgasm."

He turned to look at her, even though she hadn't yet given him permission to do so.

She gave him a smug, leonine smirk. "Maybe I'll let you give me several."

He felt himself getting hard again.

"Maybe I'll even let *you* come."

"Don't tease me," he said gruffly. "I have a meeting in ten minutes."

"Hmm... maybe I'll let you come inside me. Would you like that, Mishka?"

"Blyat," he cursed softly. He was hard as iron again. "Katya, you are a terrorist."

She laughed. "But you love it. Come here."

He went to her on his knees, slipping between her spread thighs. She wrapped her legs around his hips, drawing him in close, kissing him deeply. He gripped the arms of the chair as she savored him. The sweet intensity of that kiss told him everything he needed to know—that he was loved, that he was needed, that he was *hers*. When she finally broke away, she pressed one more kiss to his forehead, and simply stroked his hair. He let his eyes fall closed, relishing the gentle comfort of her touch.

"I love you," she whispered against the shell of his ear.

He shivered, a trail of goosebumps running down his spine. "I love you, too," he answered easily, truly.

After a quiet moment, she released him and got up from the chair. "I suppose you should get back to work." She ruffled his hair, as she walked away. Pausing in the doorway, she glanced back at him. "Oh, and remember tonight we have game night at Anna and Jason's."

"I would rather play chess with you in our own home," Mikhail grumbled as he righted his clothing. He didn't particularly crave friendship, but for Kate's sake, he tolerated her friends and did his best to be tolerable in return.

"I know you would. But we're playing euchre with six other people, so prepare yourself." She started to leave and then swung back. "If it's any consolation, I'm pretty sure that the more people that get added to these game nights, the more Jason wants to fake his own death and run away to live in the mountains."

"He would never leave—not as long as Anna is still here." Kate's gaze softened fondly. "Yeah. He loves her."

"We're victims of the same madness."

"You love Anna too?" Kate teased.

"You know who I'm talking about," he growled, catching her before she could pull the door open and pinning her against it.

"You are being very insubordinate right now," she told him sternly, while her eyes glimmered with humor.

"Are you going to punish me?"

"I might have to." She reached up to cup his face, pulling him down for a brief kiss. "But you have a meeting to get to. So, shoo." She herded him away from the door and finally let herself out, sauntering back to her domain on the floor just below his—where the Domovoy Charitable Foundation offices were housed.

He knew when she was back at her desk because his phone buzzed with an incoming message. She'd sent him a screenshot of a custom-made necklace from a high-end jeweler's social media page. Huge emeralds and rubies set in clusters that looked like flowers and leaves, meant to wrap around a woman's neck like a glittering garden.

Get me this.

The description says it's a custom piece. It belongs to someone else.

That's not my problem.

He grinned.

Don't make me punish you again.

His grin broadened. She was perfect.

———

After leaving Mikhail, Kate returned to her office to get her things, and then she was on her way out of the Domovoy building to meet her sister for lunch.

Over the last few weeks, they'd been cautiously rebuilding their relationship. Mikhail confessed that it had been a conversation with Angel that had made him understand his own feelings. Though, when Kate had asked her about it, Angel pretended not to have any idea what she was talking about. So Kate gave up asking about it.

Instead, they talked about old memories—the good and the bad—and the future. Angel's sobriety seemed to be sticking, and she'd started attending group meetings at the encouragement of the co-worker who was helping her—a man she was ridiculously tight-lipped about.

"It's not like that," Angel said, uncharacteristically quiet whenever Kate brought him up. "He would never be with someone like me."

"Someone like you?" Kate echoed, bristling on behalf of the sister she was beginning to know again. "What's that mean? What kind of 'help' is this guy giving you if he makes you feel like you're—"

"Jesus, calm down," Angel begged, looking nervously around the restaurant. "He never said anything like that. But he knows I lost custody of my kids, and—"

"But you're seeing them again?" Kate interrupted.

"Yeah," Angel answered quietly. "Aunt Deb brought them to the Milwaukee zoo on Saturday, so I met them there and spent the day with them. They were... they were really happy to see me."

Kate's heart lifted. She swallowed the knot that had tightened her throat and changed the subject before either she or Angel got too emotional. Things were better between them, but they weren't perfect. "Cool. So, uh, how's work going?"

Her sister shrugged. "It's fine. And you?"

And like that, they had one of the most normal conversations they'd probably had in their entire lives thus far. At the end of lunch, Kate pretended to go to the bathroom, sneaking over to the waitress station to get the bill. Angel smacked her on the arm when she found out, called her a bitch, and then they hugged awkwardly before going their separate ways.

——

BACK AT HOME THAT NIGHT—HER NEW HOME, THE Lincoln Park mansion—she lay in bed with Mikhail, safer, happier, and more loved than she'd ever been. Her whole body was sore in the best of ways, exhausted from too many orgasms and an overly-ambitious attempt at a sex position that just wasn't possible when one partner outweighed the other by sixty pounds. Ah well. Mikhail had gotten to come inside her, and as much fun as it was to withhold that from him, it was even better to finally give in, to hold him deep inside of her, and feel his pleasure inside her body.

He was sprawled next to her now, asleep. The room was dark, with only faint moonlight to show her the edges of shapes. Her gaze traveled lazily around the darkness. That shadowed rectangle on the wall above the fireplace had once been some random eighteenth-century painting of a ship. But

Kate had replaced it with a picture of the two of them, taken on their first trip to Shanghai together.

She let her gaze drift to Mikhail, tracing along the hard lines of his face. He wasn't a perfect man. He might not even be a good man. But he lived and breathed for her happiness, and if he couldn't be a good person on his own, she could command it of him. She was alright with that—even if it called her own ethics into question.

"Mishka?" she whispered into the silence.

"Mmm?"

"I love you."

He shifted towards her, pulling her into his arms and holding her tightly. "I love you, Katya."

Also by Heather Guerre

***Lake Lenora* series:**

Contemporary Small-Town Romances

What Could Have Been

What Was Meant To Be

—

***Tooth & Claw* series:**

Paranormal Shifter and Vampire Romances

Cold Hearted

Hot Blooded

Once Bitten

—

***Hellbound* series:**

Paranormal Demon Romances

Demon Lover

—

***Forbidden Mates* series:**

Sci-fi Alien Romances

Star Crossed

Moon Struck

Heart Song

About the Author

Heather Guerre writes sexy-sweet fantasy, sci-fi, and contemporary romances. A hopeless romantic and an unapologetic nerd, Heather loves everything to do with romance, aliens, shifters, cyborgs, monsters, and magic.

For more from Heather, you can subscribe to her newsletter at heatherguerre.com/newsletter. Subscribers receive alerts for new releases as well as newsletter-exclusive bonus material.

———

bsky.app/profile/heatherguerre.bsky.social

instagram.com/authorheatherguerre

goodreads.com/heatherguerre

bookbub.com/authors/heather-guerre